PAOLA CAPRIOLO was born ~~~~~~~~~~~ ~~~~~ she now lives. Her first bo~~~~~~~~~~~~~~~~ collection of short stories, ~~~~~~~~~~~~~~~~~ Berto Prize. *Il nocciero*, a novel, won the 1990 Rapallo Prize and in 1991 she was awarded the Förder Prize in Germany for her work. Her second novel, *Vissi d'amore*, was published in 1992; it was translated by Liz Heron and published by Serpent's Tail in 1997 as *Floria Tosca*. Paola Capriolo is a translator and writes for the cultural pages of *Il Corriere Della Sera*.

Also by Paula Capriolo and published by Serpent's Tail

Floria Tosca
Translated by Liz Heron

Praise for *Floria Tosca*

'In this brilliant novel, the Milanese writer Paola Capriolo doesn't so much retell the story of Puccini's opera "Tosca" as invent a document inspired by it. . . . This shift in focus enables a shrewd and stylish adaptation that also works independently of the opera. . . . An essential part of this novel's success is Capriolo's elegant writing, a highly readable evocation of 19th-century Italian prose style. The British writer Liz Heron fashions a remarkably suggestive English version that never fails to match Capriolo's archaisms and often adds to them with inventive choices. . . . Heron's translation manages to be both artful and absorbing. It compels the recognition that very little in the English-language Gothic tradition can compare with the sheer intellectual sophistication of Paolo Capriolo's novel.' *New York Times Book Review*

'Capriolo's elegant and precise narrative adds a cruel, psychological intensity to the story, and the result is an exhilarating tale of fatal attraction.' *The Good Book Guide*

'Capriolo creates a mood of gothic darkness and a deep sense of sexual unease in this minimalist tour-de-force.' *The Irish Times*

THE WOMAN
WATCHING

PAOLA CAPRIOLO

✤

translated by Liz Heron

Library of Congress Catalog Card Number: 98–84075

A complete catalogue record for this book can be
obtained from the British Library on request

The right of Paola Capriolo to be identified as the author
of this work has been asserted by her in accordance
with the Copyright, Designs and Patents Act 1988

First published in Italian as *La spettatrice* in 1995 by Bompiani, Milan
Copyright © 1995 R.C.S. Libri + Grandi Opere S.p.A.

Translation copyright © 1998 Liz Heron

This edition first published in 1998 by
Serpent's Tail, 4 Blackstock Mews, London N4

Phototypeset in 11pt Garamond by Intype London Ltd
Printed in Great Britain by Mackays of Chatham, plc

10 9 8 7 6 5 4 3 2 1

to my parents

NO ONE CAN SAY for certain how Vulpius came to meet his fate, nor what occurrences, reflections and obsessions marked its progress. It was never vouchsafed to either friends or colleagues to unlock the mystery of that soul, and she who perhaps examined it most closely is now no longer able to give us her testimony. Opinions are divided even on Vulpius's real nature, the meaning of his actions and the motives that determined them; some try to explain those incomprehensible goings-on as the ultimate outcome of despair, others put them down to some seed of madness that gradually grew within his mind and finally overwhelmed it entirely.

It is easy enough to be swayed by one or other of these interpretations, harder to reconstruct the unfolding of events. Even what I am about to narrate is only one possible story of Vulpius, in which the few indisputable elements which we have available can be accounted for. I would not go so far as to maintain that this is then his true story, or even the most likely one; the life of this individual seems to have proceeded in such a way as to invalidate any criterion of verisimilitude, and if ever any kind of truth appeared in it, it would have had to be a disturbing and paradoxical one, almost unrecognisable beneath the varicoloured raiment of fiction.

Let us, then, imagine this possible story. Let us submit reality itself to the purifying process required by literary invention, which is so much more rigorous, so much more demanding in the matter of essentials and coherence, and let us imagine a quiet town, which is neither big nor small, and whose name and location on the map we have no need to know; in short, a possible town, in which for now there are only two buildings of interest to us. The first of these is the theatre, once a court theatre, now municipal, a rococo casket all crimson velvets and gilded stucco, where, every evening, for nine months of the year, the permanent company entertains those citizens who wish to be entertained with programmes in which something is accorded to novelty, and much to custom. Every evening, at nine on the dot, the chandeliers that hang over the stalls gradually dim, the orchestra dutifully lends its own voice to the atmosphere of anticipation which is deemed to reign over the hall, and when even the coat of arms that dominates the stage, held aloft by two plumplimbed cupids, has completely vanished into the darkness, the curtain finally rises to reveal sets which are perhaps not greatly unexpected, but executed with taste and with no expense spared.

Farces, tragedies and the countless intervening

forms which the theatrical tradition has been able to devise between the two extremes of laughter and torment, alternate upon the boards of the stage, in a style usually appreciated by those few cognoscenti present in the hall above all for its unstinting diligence and admirable moderation of tone. The uninitiated, however, who make up the overwhelming majority of regular theatregoers, exchange their own opinions after the performance with mutual expressions of delighted wonderment that it all seemed so real and that they themselves, thanks to the power of dramatic illusion, had felt tears spring to their eyes at the sad fate of the heroine, or had experienced the keenest satisfaction at the final ignominy of the insufferable old miser. Among the spectators of this sort, the events represented on the stage produce the fellow-feeling of those who have gone on a long journey together, fought side by side in some memorable battle or shared some other adventure, and the comments, interpretations, criticisms and praise addressed to the conduct of the various characters continue at length in the square adjacent to the theatre long after all the lights have gone out and it seems impossible that behind its dark façade such distant worlds can have opened up, such singular goings-on unfolded. Then even the last knots of people scatter, and, as a rule, once half past twelve has passed a deep silence soon pervades the square.

So the curtain has come down, the actors have long since taken off their costumes and their heavy stage make-up and left the theatre dressed in everyday clothes or at most something only a little outlandish. If we want to keep track of the characters in our story, we must turn our attention to the second of the two buildings I mentioned above, a small boarding-house, not far from the theatre, where the company has made its home for years. In the ground-floor dining-room, which can also be reached from the street, the actors gather after the play to have a lavish supper together. It is a plain, comfortable little room, where there is nothing to recall the baroque pomposity of the former court theatre, apart from the decidedly theatrical inclinations evinced by the cook in the way the dishes are presented: sliced vegetables in bright colours are fanned out round the roasts, the dessert trolley displays tall peaks of whipped cream and constellations of meringues and little cherries, and not even a plain steak or slice of cheese is brought to the table without its simple nutritional function being refined and transfigured by some adornment.

For the most part such zeal turns out to be a wasted effort, since no sooner are these actors out of the theatre than they seem suddenly to lose all interest in form, caring merely for substance, as befits the principles of a sound pragmatism. Firmly brandishing their forks, they demolish the cook's complex architectural structures; pitilessly, they push aside the curly lettuce leaves and wedges of lemon; ruthlessly, they reduce the chromatic balance of chocolate and cream to the most undifferentiated mess. There is only one of them, a young actress, who has a moment's hesitation, pausing to let her mesmerised gaze dwell on those marvels almost as if she were tasting them with her eyes first before her palate did, and invariably giving a faint sigh when the time comes to destroy them. 'It's so beautiful,' she says, 'that it's just a shame to eat it,' but then she eats it all up heartily, down to the last morsel.

Perhaps there are some who still remember her name. Not the name she was born with, of course, but the vaguely exotic professional name with which she had replaced it, a name of the kind that is hard to locate among the saints in the calendar, but one which, to a naive girl who has grown up in a small town, has the semblance of conferring an air of gentility and mystery upon its bearer.

I think I shall baptise the young actress with the name Dora; it may be her real name, it is certainly a likely one, and with this character we can move with full assurance upon the terrain of verisimilitude. Her whole demeanour conveys a healthy, carefree confidence in the pleasures of life, and a total unfamiliarity with any of its morbid or complicated aspects. A rare, perhaps non-existent nature, which, however, once transposed into the domain of fiction, becomes a very common, not to say banal, one, as if healthiness of this kind constituted the norm for human beings.

A task that turns out to be much more difficult is that of describing the character sitting opposite her, the young actor who treads the boards under the name Vulpius. For now he remains an opaque figure, unknown to us as he is to himself, even if within

5

that figure there lurks in latent form the whole development of our story. Perhaps something of it can be guessed at by noting the pallor of his face, which contrasts so much with the girl's rosy complexion, or the premature little wrinkles which almost imperceptibly line his brow. He is sociable, affable with his colleagues and especially so with Dora; the most we can observe from his bearing is a very faint touch of distance, an unconscious sense of not feeling at home among those who surround him.

It is irrelevant whether we know anything of his origins or his previous life. As far as we are concerned, Vulpius is born at this moment, as we see him sitting among his colleagues at the boarding-house table, or perhaps he is not born yet, he is only a foreboding of himself, and his being will acquire firmly defined outlines only with the progressive definition of his fate. In the meantime, the things we need to know about this hazy individual are few: that he is young, that he resembles the others but is not the same, that he is in love with Dora and that she reciprocates.

Considering him to be in love is still taking too much for granted. We do not know him well enough yet, and it would be downright presumption to claim we can read the mind of a stranger at first sight. I shall therefore go no further than to say that every night, after the actors had retired, Vulpius would go out into the corridor in his dressing-gown and pyjamas and knock on Dora's door, from under which a sliver of light still crept. Sometimes he would stay there until morning and the two of them would breakfast together in the drawing-room next to the bedroom. It was seldom enough that Dora made her way to his room; in fact she could not abide the fastidious tidiness that prevailed there. Vulpius had added nothing to its sober furnishings; every evening, before joining Dora, he would carefully hang up his clothes in the wardrobe, every morning he would throw the newspapers into the waste basket immediately after reading them, and he never left a book off the shelf; in short, he lived in that room as if he wished to hide the traces of his presence from someone. Dora, on the other hand, loved cluttering her own room with scarves and little hats, magazines and boxes of sweets, and on top of the chest of drawers she had built a kind of household altar around the portraits of her dead parents, and here and there had stuck playbills and on-stage photographs on the old wallpaper. For all this she could not be called slovenly; in her, even untidiness was always ruled by some instinctive grace, and seemed a natural demonstration of a temperament that was alien from any manner of severity.

This characteristic also determined the style of her performance, which, according to the considered collective verdict issued by the cognoscenti, was never without a shade of amateurishness, although they were disposed to forgive her this for the sake of her lovely luminous face and her firm and shapely figure, which was always shown off to good effect by her costumes, and they would usually refer to these endowments with the somewhat vague expression 'stage presence'.

As for Vulpius, it was his good fortune to have almost nothing that needed be forgiven him. He was regarded as an actor who was not yet mature, but very promising, and the cognoscenti benevolently followed the sure ascent which led him to ever more important roles. In common with the case of the beautiful Dora, here too they wished to make it very plain that their opinion, though it did indeed, by some peculiar quirk, coincide with that of the wider audience, was dictated by quite different reasons. What in Vulpius was admired above all by the ignorant masses was in fact his capacity to ensnare them completely in illusion, almost erasing the boundary between himself and the character. When he died on stage it seemed to them that he was really dying, and they shifted uneasily in their seats; tears, laughter, rage and amorous passion, everything that Vulpius simulated on the stage possessed in their eyes the chrism of truth, of the most authentic nature. They were disconcerted each time they saw him change from one evening to the next from a dramatic role to a comic one, from the part of a good man to that of the villain, as if he were thereby revealing some incomprehensible mutability in his being; but every time, after just a few lines, they would become wholly engrossed in the new fiction, convincing themselves that this was just how he was, that Vulpius – who would ever have thought it – was just that type; or, rather, they no longer gave a thought to Vulpius, since before their eyes there

stood in the flesh Pylades or Iago, Puck or Harlequin.

Let us imagine this young chameleon, with the
curtain just fallen on the final bows, on his way to
the dressing-rooms with his fellow actors. He sits
down at the dressing-table to take off his make-
up, his hand executing swift, deft movements, and
perhaps something flits across his face, the dim
reflection of an idea that vanishes at once. He looks
at himself absentmindedly in the mirror, all the while
conversing with his colleagues, or with a member of
the audience who has come to congratulate him, or
with Dora, who always remains Dora whatever role
she is performing and without ever making her exit
from the stage experiencing that dizziness which is
so like a rude awakening. It is a feeling of estrangement, of not-belonging, which keeps hold for a
while even outside the theatre, while Vulpius travels
the short distance to the boarding-house together
with the others, and it sometimes still has him in its
grip even at table, the whole evening long, faint yet
discernible, and it is only in the depths of the night,
in Dora's room, that it slowly leaves him.

THE ACTORS' LIVES PROCEEDED with precise regularity, in a manner no less ordered than the rules of
bourgeois life, and with no resemblance whatsoever
to the adventurous one led by travelling players.
Many of them had wound up at the municipal
theatre after years of performing in touring companies, but now they seemed to have buried for ever
any memory of former ways, just like those who,
having risen in the social scale beyond their expectations, deny their humble origins. Each of them
possessed a scroll of thick, watermarked paper
which, in fluttering italic script, conferred on them
the title of Actor of the Municipal Theatre – not a
lofty title, yet an enviable one, and these papers,
duly framed, occupied the place of honour on the
walls of their bedrooms. Anyone entering would
encounter them directly, as if the inhabitant of the
room wanted to make things quite plain at once, so
that the visitor would be well aware of whom he
was dealing with and behave accordingly, and its

PAOLA CAPRIOLO

owner would himself readily pause to contemplate
this document which he perceived as the guarantee
of a dignified future free of anxieties. Only in Vulpius's bedroom was the diploma not displayed but
kept in a drawer among other papers; yet his colleagues had never had the chance to wonder or
enquire about such eccentricity, since the young man
never received anyone in his own room, except
Dora, and when she was with Vulpius she paid no
great attention to the walls.

Otherwise, our protagonist, too, adjusted without
reservations to the mild discipline which governed
the lives of the company, to the routines that marked
it, the repetition of gestures, words, even thoughts,
thus faithfully reproducing each day the same, perpetual script. Perhaps one might even venture to
suppose that he saw a certain peculiar charm in these
serene rituals, to which the others yielded almost
unconsciously, regarding them as a mere corollary
to their status as Municipal Actors.

Let us raise the curtain on one such day. It will
not unfold very differently from usual, and yet in
the eyes of the actors it has special significance,
because this very evening the theatre will re-open
its doors after the summer closure. It is two weeks
now since the boarding house filled up again; the
actors have already had enough of swapping stories
of their holidays, visits to relatives, restful stays in
the countryside or in some moderately priced resort,
and they have had time to ascertain with satisfaction
that during their absence nothing has altered, the
bedrooms are still clean and neat and quiet, the

dishes prepared by the cook as tasty as ever and served with generous helpings. Thus reassured about the solid props of their existence, they can immerse themselves once more in the calm flux of routine.

That morning Dora was the first to wake, and after throwing over her shoulders a blue dressing-gown trimmed with ostrich feathers, she tiptoed over to the French window. She inched back the curtains, letting a sliver of light enter the room. It was a beautiful day, the sunlight spread across the rooftops of the town, and against the cloudless sky the great copper dome of the church stood out in sharp relief, strangely near. Dora was gladdened by this sight; like many actors, she was apt to be super-stitious and she would interpret whatever happened around her as a series of happy or woeful portents, almost as if some secret correspondence prevailed between the progress of the world and the humble events of her life; so the fact that the season was probably not destined to be launched in the rain was taken by her as a sign of benevolence on the part of whatever entity governed both of these. She addressed a moment's thought of fervent gratitude to this entity; she was indeed aware that even the most munificent of benefactors should from time to time be flattered in order that his feelings are not dampened, and that the best weapon in the hands of a beneficiary desirous of receiving further benefits is acknowledgement. 'I thank you for what you're doing for me,' the look in her eyes said, as it became lost in the vague distance beyond the greenish glare of the dome, 'only, see you don't let me down the next time.'

Then Dora's reflections took a more practical turn; with the weather so mild, she thought, we could have breakfast outside, on the little terrace. She looked back inside the room. Vulpius was still asleep, on his back, the sheet completely wrapped round him. That night his sleep had been disturbed, which had amazed Dora, since the approach of a first night had never given him the slightest anxiety before; now, however, he was lying in that still, extraordinarily composed, almost rigid, pose which was customary for him and which Dora could never look upon without dismay. Though she saw his form as pleasant and attractive when Vulpius was awake, that sleeping body always aroused in her an inexplicable revulsion. In that face she could not recognise the features of her sweetheart, her affectionate companion, familiar as they were; it was cold, alien, even inhuman, it seemed sculpted from marble, and its pallor was all the starker without the compensatory brilliance of his large dark eyes.

Normally Dora made light of any displeasing impression, any disturbing element that arose in her relationship with Vulpius; but she had never said a word about this strange uneasiness, and she herself dwelt on it as little as possible, swiftly dispelling it like some nightmare soon forgotten on awakening.

When she had looked at the grandfather clock that hung on one wall of the little drawing-room and realised that it was some time after eleven, she put an end to her idling and with a feeling of relief opened wide all the curtains. Wounded by the light, Vulpius's face contracted, and, rousing himself from his torpor, he raised an arm to shield his eyes.

In a tone of humorous indignation Dora asked him if he knew what time it was. How could I know? he retorted, and added that he was prepared to accept whatever relevant information Dora might wish to supply on this question. Yet once he had received it he stayed in bed without stirring himself, while she rang the bell to have breakfast brought, and only when he heard the knock on the door did he rise and withdraw behind the screen.

Certainly, everyone living under that roof was well aware of their connection, but, perhaps from regard for bourgeois prejudices, or perhaps for the sake of her own dignity as a municipal actress, Dora carefully avoided making it public, and went so far as to compel the young man to some manner of subterfuge every time there was need for an attendant to set foot in the room.

On leaving his hiding-place, Vulpius found breakfast served at the table on the little terrace and his friend wholly engaged in the difficult task of choosing between a brioche and a small pot of marmalade. Finally Dora took the little pot and with a resolute air went off to place it in a cabinet which was already overflowing with provisions of the kind she termed 'comforters'; then she went back to the terrace, lightened of the burden of decision, and dipped the brioche in her milky coffee.

Had Vulpius noticed what a lovely day it was? Yes, of course, he had noticed. And wasn't he also sure that the first night would be a triumph? The actor answered this enquiry with a faint smile; the link between weather conditions and successful performances seemed to elude him utterly, as with the intricate network of premonitory hints which Dora viewed as enveloping reality. He did not even make the sign of the cross before a stage entrance, even though it was a simple precaution which she had often advised him to adopt.

Yet today Vulpius too looked at the view outside with interest. He was especially enchanted by the glittering dome of the church, and extolled the masterly illusion whereby the sun's rays stripped its metallic surface of all solidity, transforming it into a play of reflections, a conflagration without movement.

She countered that it was this very brilliance which she found intolerable; it was a lovely sight, without doubt, but it was blinding. And then, why fix so firmly upon one point alone, when the view below them opened out so amply and generously, offering such a great variety of attractions? The towers, for instance, and the tall spires which here and there rose up from the compact mass of the town, or the hills, so restful still in their summer apparel, specked with only occasional patches of brown here and there . . . Vulpius acquiesced absent-mindedly, but his gaze settled again and again on the great copper dome.

At last Dora got up from her little easy chair and dragged him away from that contemplation. It's not so warm as I thought, she said, bringing a hand to her breast to close the neckline of her dressing-gown. She went back into the bedroom, and after a few moments he followed her.

LET US PICTURE THE actors, with their first night approaching, going through the day in the grip of a faint anxiety which nevertheless fails to modify their now well-established daily routines. At one on the dot they all gather in the restaurant, including Dora and Vulpius, she excited, he calm and absorbed, and as course after course of the meal celebrates its ephemeral triumph, each of them tries to corner the attention of the leading actor, whose job is also that of director, to explain to him some problem that has come up at the last minute in an umpteenth, solitary revision of their respective parts. The leading actor gives each of them fleeting reassurance and puts off all commentary until the general rehearsal set for that afternoon, as usual, from three until six. Let us not mix the sacred and profane, is his brusque exhortation as he bites into his chicken leg; an ambiguous phrase, given that it is almost impossible to establish which in his eyes is the sacred and which the profane. At any rate, no one dares object;

whether out of respect or even from being awed by that man with his powerful voice and hearty appetite, I could not say, or because in the eyes of the questioners themselves their difficulties do not seem so serious as to have to be discussed over lunch, disrupting the serene progress of such a fundamental ritual.

Whichever play has been selected for the opening performance, we can assume that it is no novelty for the company. In all likelihood some success from the previous season has been dusted down, so as to take no chances; we should remember that the Municipal Actors are not adventurers, their heads are set firmly on their shoulders, and their options are always thought through with extreme caution. Reviving a limited repertoire every year and taking it to that point of perfection allowed by the artistic skills within their group is as much as one can legitimately expect of them, and it is no small thing, it has to be said; in the long run one ends up valuing such circumspection in fashioning a programme when one has become weary of watching those unfortunate experiments attempted by companies which are less wise and more uninhibited.

It sometimes happens that a young playwright who is full of himself pesters the actor-manager asking him at least to read his work and then, if possible, stage it, or that one of the cognoscenti, back from a trip, enthuses about the extraordinary critical success reaped in another theatre by some new piece or the bold resurrection of some forgotten classic. 'If people want to give themselves a hard time of it,' the leading actor answers drily, 'they're welcome, but we're having nothing to do with it.' For his part, he considers himself responsible for his colleagues like a good father for his children, and the basic duty he must fulfil is the protection of all those in his trust from the risk of making themselves ridiculous in front of the whole town. These same criteria guide his decisions about production and performance, which are unfailingly praised in the authoritative columns of the local newspaper for their 'exemplary classicism', and if it is suggested to him, for example, that Richard III should be played as anything other than a hunchback or that there should be no on-stage burst of hellfire flames at the end of *Don Juan*, he does not even reply, but merely smiles as if confronted by some perverse humorist's facetious remark. Should his interlocutor labour the point, he wastes no time in cutting the conversation short with the assertion that he is not obliged to account to anyone for his choices, except to the municipal superintendent and his own conscience.

With all this in mind, it is understandable that the actors should feel that they are home and dry and that anticipation of the opening night should fail to upset their healthy interest in the pleasures of the table. After lunch, therefore, they went up to their rooms with their minds at rest to take their afternoon nap, and shortly before three they reassembled in the hall to make their way calmly to the theatre.

Since we have mentioned *Don Juan*, we might suppose that this was the very play scheduled for that evening. The role of the unrepentant libertine had for years been the actor-manager's forte, and the fact that his figure had grown somewhat stouter and the auburn shade of his hair was preserved only by artificial means did not seem to him to undermine in any substantial way his credibility in the guise of that irresistible conqueror of women's hearts. Besides, the leading actress who, heavily and opaquely veiled, would play the part of Doña Elvira, was not much younger than him, and, according to her fellow actresses, she had to be grateful for the impenetrability of her costume if her consort's desertion was not to provoke the audience's perception that the reasons were well founded. Dora alone abstained from such malicious observations, perhaps because her somewhat under-ambitious nature made any kind of envy alien to her. She was an actress from love of the actress's life, and she was almost indifferent to whichever role came her way, so long as it allowed her to submit her own natural endowments to public scrutiny. In Doña Elvira's severe apparel she would have felt quite mortified, while the part of the peasant girl Charlotte, although a modest one, let her show off a costume which, besides suiting her wonderfully, in no way detracted from her beauty by concealing it any more than was strictly necessary.

Instead, Dora focused her artistic ambitions entirely on Vulpius, in whose gifts and future successes she maintained unconditional faith, and so she was most happy that he had been assigned a role as important as that of Sganarelle. Of course, logic and justice dictated that her sweetheart should have played the part of Don Juan, it would have been a huge advantage for the production if the part of the seductive libertine had gone to Vulpius instead of to that clapped-out ham actor, and she herself would have had much more fun yielding to his seduction on-stage. But the principle 'Make the best of what you have' was indelibly stamped upon Dora's soul; it had protected her more than once in the past from an unpleasant sense of disappointment and now too it came to her aid, allowing her to face the evening with no trace of rancour or ill-humour.

So the play was performed from start to finish with the stalls almost empty; the superintendent sat alone in the middle of the third row paying a great deal of attention to the costumes and sets, and he did not judge the money allocated to that production to have been ill-spent. It was necessary, however, to forgo rehearsal of the special effects in the final scene, given the absence of the fire brigade, which would not arrive in the theatre before eight. This meant that Don Juan's collapse into the infernal abyss was reduced to a circumspectly executed little jump by the leading actor into a not-very-deep trap-door opened out on to the stage, while the flames, clouds of vapour and solemn accompaniment of thunder and lightning were left to the superintend-ent's imagination, which was not one of the most lively.

Yet, when the punished dissolute re-emerged from the trapdoor after Sganarelle's last line, and the other actors came out from behind the scenes, it was all mutual congratulations on how well the rehearsal had gone, and the superintendent too expressed his own satisfaction with a moderate degree of warmth. Then he took his watch out of his waistcoat pocket and after consulting it hastily took his leave, urging the actors to allow themselves a little rest before returning to the theatre at eight o'clock sharp.

Despite the general deference towards this authoritative personage, almost no one followed his advice. To rest two hours away from an opening was an undertaking beyond human powers, and to most of them even leaving the theatre seemed a pointless effort. The actor-manager withdrew to his own dressing-room to wait for eight o'clock with the pleasant distraction of a bottle of spirits and a few colleagues faithful to his doctrine whereby being on stage requires neither complete drunkenness nor complete sobriety. Disciples of this school included, among others, the austere Doña Elvira and the stone guest, whose cheeks very quickly took on a rubicund complexion; but this did not worry him, since it would only take a thick layer of white greasepaint to restore to his face the marmoreal pallor indispensable to the role. In Dora's dressing-room, the three young actresses sought similar comfort in a large box of chocolates, the gift of an admirer, and every so often they would turn an enquiring glance towards the mirror in order to receive confirmation of their unaltered attractiveness.

Vulpius had tried in vain to persuade Dora to accompany him on a short walk, and at last he had gone out alone. He strolled through the streets of the town centre, with no definite goal, taking deep breaths of the fresh evening air in which there was already a hint of winter to come. It was not yet dark, but in the main thoroughfares the lamplight was mingled with twilight, and in the sky a diaphanous sickle of moon faced out the dying sun.

We do not know what Vulpius's thoughts were, nor for what reason he had felt the need to leave the theatre and undertake that solitary walk; we might believe that in movement he sought an outlet for his own impatience, were this hypothesis not contradicted by the positively phlegmatic calm with which he traversed those familiar streets and now and then paused to look at a fountain, a picturesque shop sign or the architecture of a building. One would have thought him a traveller passing through and engaged on a brief tour of the town to kill time between one train and the next, looking around with detached curiosity, following this or that direction as chance dictated or the whim took him.

In this way, almost without realising, he got as far as the church, the same church he had gazed upon that morning from the terrace with Dora. He cast a glance of absentminded approval upon the sinuous lines of the façade, and was about to go on when the main door opened to let out a group of the faithful, and for a moment he glimpsed a glitter of gold inside. He had never set foot in that church, although he had passed by it many times, but now he felt himself strangely attracted and without hesitation stepped through the main door.

The great oval space beneath the arch of the dome was empty; not one single ray of light fell from above, but the long rows of candles lit before the altars sent out a reddish glimmer, disclosing the rich decorations on the walls in which the symbols of earthly splendour were entwined with those of death. Garlands and cherubs, illumined by the tiny flames, flickered fuzzily, while among them, at intervals, the white of a skull stood out distinctly, almost glaring, and a statue armed with a scythe bent over the holy water font in a gesture which called to mind not so much the threat of annihilation as the polite obeisance of a courtier. In that funereal splendour lavished on every part of the church there was in fact a trace of vanity, of worldly display, even of voluptuous abandon, and at the base of the dome the seven angels who announced the day of judgement with their trumpets seemed to be the heralds of a seductive and incomprehensible revel.

Vulpius had completely shed the demeanour of the dreamy tourist; now he looked all around with his brow slightly furrowed as if from the effort of grasping a thought which continued to elude him. He was so engrossed that when the great door opened at his back and clicked shut again the sudden noise made him start. He turned and saw an elegant middle-aged lady approach the altar, leading a little girl by the hand. It seemed to Vulpius that he knew her, or at least someone who looked like her; she might be the wife or the widow of some highly placed functionary or professional man, a member of the best society, a regular attender at every kind of launch or opening and first nights at the theatre. She was dressed in the height of fashion, with even a touch of the trendsetter, which was something seldom encountered in a town so reluctant as this one to welcome innovation; the little girl, probably her daughter, was instead attired in a more classical style, one suitably in keeping with her age and the standing of her parents.

When she was a few steps away from the altar, the woman let go of the child's hand and in a sudden vigorous movement she bent one knee to the ground while her arm traced a swift, sure sign of the cross. Vulpius watched this gesture, which was so ancient and so solemn, so much in contrast with the lady's up-to-date elegance. He was amazed and admiring, faintly amused. 'Very good,' he said softly, with an expert's cool approval. 'Almost perfect.'

The child had imitated her mother, though without being able to match her spontaneity; they remained side by side on their knees, their heads bowed, absorbed in a silent prayer. Carefully, so as not to disturb them, Vulpius made his way to the door and went out, closing it slowly behind him.

NOW THE THEATRE WAS crowded with men and women who lingered chatting in the foyer, wandered up and down the aisles of the stalls looking for their seats or leaned out of boxes to wave to some acquaintance. As ever, on the opening night none of the more prominent townspeople was missing, and the gossip columnist from the local paper roamed about tirelessly taking note of how the ladies were dressed. Silk and satin, long feather boas and super-abundantly-stranded necklaces produced on this side of the curtain a spectacle even more lavish than the one that was soon to be presented behind it, and triumphantly offered a theme on which in the coming days a series of discussions and commentaries would be developed like an elaborate symphony.

When the lights dimmed as the first warning, almost nobody appeared to take any notice. The second time, however, they complied, but the majority were secretly annoyed, and many regarded it as downright impertinence to interrupt other people's conversation in so high-handed a manner. Only the cognoscenti took their seats gladly, anticipating the pleasant and always gratifying exercise of their critical faculties, even more than the performance itself.

The buzz continued while the orchestra tuned up, but when the lights went out all voices were hushed; these moments of darkness and silence marked the passage from reality to fiction. Everyone had focused their attention and concentration, discarding their own thoughts, their own interests, their own personality, and, as if by a miracle, that frivolous and chattering company became transformed into an audience.

At last the orchestra began playing some music that was grave at first, then cheerful, and the curtain rose to reveal the interior of a princely palace of the kind that can be imagined by those who have never lived in one. Sganarelle, standing in the centre of the stage, held a small silver box in his hand, and after curtly acknowledging the applause that greeted him he began to exalt the social and moral merits of tobacco to Doña Elvira's valet. The audience were laughing; at that initial point they could still manage to distinguish Vulpius from Sganarelle, and whispering, they exchanged laudatory remarks on the skill of the characterisation, in particular the young actor's physical posture, which was at all times somewhat stiff, with a curving of the back, as if he had never done anything else in his life but bow from left to right or dodge the blows of a despotic master, and on the circumspect air with which, all the while in tones of smug indignation expounding Don Juan's wickedness to his interlocutor, he looked over his shoulder in fear of being surprised by the former.

But no one noticed that Vulpius took advantage of this pantomime to inspect the audience. He could tell at a glance that, though the house was not full, it at least came close. There was not a single empty seat left in the stalls and the boxes were occupied for the most part, including the royal box in which sat the mayor with his much-bejewelled spouse and a few select guests. The elderly chief critic and the editor of the newspaper had been invited as usual to the superintendent's box, for he took it upon himself to take personal care of relations with the press. Wherever his gaze came to rest, Vulpius discerned only familiar faces, and it could be that this circumstance produced in him a faint sense of tedium.

Meanwhile the valet had left the stage and the leading actor had made his entrance, to a welcome of thunderous applause. Many of those present had memories of his performing Don Juan that went as far back as their youth, and now it gave them satisfaction to greet what seemed to them a venerable custom and also an exceedingly comforting proof of how time had gone by since those days without devastating results. Naturally, compared with twenty years earlier their Don Juan had put on a bit of weight, his movements were not quite so nimble as once they had been, his voice now had less richness in its timbre, yet it had to be allowed that he still carried himself very well and this was perfectly to be expected anyway, since after all twenty years don't make an eternity, neither for actors nor for ordinary citizens. So they were all too willing to put their imaginations fully to work to dissipate the sense of incongruity that was prompted by the elderly seducer's arrogant declarations of principle, a man who still deemed his own heart fit to love the entire world and still viewed as realistic his goal of flight from one victory to the next, extending his amorous conquests as did Alexander his military ones.

When these boasts and more were cut off by the entrance of a wrathful Doña Elvira, Vulpius withdrew to a corner of the stage to enjoy a short respite. It relaxed him to feel that the audience's attention was no longer upon him; yet, while the leading actress said her lines he still had the sensation, no, the certainty, of being watched. Covertly he examined the hall from top to bottom, until his eyes met those of a woman sitting alone in a proscenium box. Vulpius was sure he had never seen her before. She looked very young, and contrary to the dictates of fashion she wore her hair long and loose on her shoulders. In the shadows her features could scarcely be made out; only her large black eyes seemed to shine with a light of their own, and were stubbornly fixed on Vulpius, as if there was no one but him in the entire theatre.

As he heard Don Juan addressing him all of a sudden, he was visibly jolted in a way that was not altogether acting. For a moment he seemed to have

forgotten his lines, so that the prompter was about
to intervene, but he rallied at once and delivered
them faultlessly. Laughter and applause rose from
the hall in strict compliance with his expectations,
almost as if he had been the one to command them,
and the rest of that act went without a hitch until
the curtain came down.

During the scene-change, Vulpius went back to
his dressing-room. The actors to-ed and fro-ed
breathlessly, and a commotion of loud voices could
be heard all along the corridor, but he remained
distanced from these perturbations. He sat down in
front of the mirror to adjust his make-up, and his
thoughts continued to return to the woman
glimpsed in the box; when Dora stopped on her way
to the stage and put her head round the door for
some last-minute reassurance, all he did was give her
vague good wishes. For a little while he heard
her muttering complicated incantations as she
walked away; then, muffled in the distance, the
popular tune struck up by the orchestra heralded
the start of the second act. Now the commotion had
abated, and the comings and goings had also become
less frequent. Vulpius was glad that he was allowed
a few moments of calm before his entrance, because
he dimly perceived the necessity to concentrate and
reflect. His eyes rested on the mirror, inspecting
his own image with punctilious care; he wondered
whatever could have stirred such keen interest in
that woman, but was unable to find a satisfactory
answer, although in general he was aware of his
power to exercise a certain charm on female sensibil-

ities. Repeatedly he affected Sganarelle's comic facial expressions, he made his back curve and hunched his neck into his shoulders; then he straightened up again, smiling and shaking his head.

The stage manager's peremptory banging on the door dragged him out of this vain puzzlement. He hurriedly tidied his costume, donned his hat again, setting it askew, and went back up on-stage behind Don Juan. Some time went by before he was able to cast a glance towards the proscenium box; the unknown woman was still in her seat and still staring at him with that strange insistence, which both flattered him and provoked an increasing anxiety. Because of her gaze it seemed to him that he was alone on stage, delivering for her a long monologue in which the pauses and silences and the moments of stillness assumed the same importance as the gestures and the words. It was a role whose meaning and nature eluded him, but which did not correspond to the one set out in the script; alongside the plot of *Don Juan* another, secret one was unfolding, only intersecting it at sporadic moments, and it was the watching woman who held its threads in her hand.

In the third act, Sganarelle had to conceal himself behind a cardboard bush in order to avoid a group of armed men. In that position he was hidden from the majority of the public, but the unknown woman, from her box, could still see him. Although his view of her face remained indistinct, Vulpius had the impression that she was smiling at him, perhaps because now the large black eyes shone, or so it

seemed to him, with a light that was singularly
sweet. At any rate, he wanted to return that hypo-
thetical smile, and meanwhile offered the hint of a
bow. She did not move, gave no reaction. She
appeared to have understood his bow not as a real
greeting but as part of the play; despite their sustained exchange of looks, there persisted between
them that uncrossable boundary which separates the
actor from the member of the audience, and as soon
as he understood this Vulpius abandoned his attempt
to establish any personal communication with her.

He continued staring at her as the dialogue being
worked through on the stage reached him from afar,
as though it belonged to a different reality. His contemplation of the unknown woman drew close
around him a veil which words and sounds scarcely
penetrated, and when he heard the voice of Don
Juan call him back to the scene, at first he did not
even realise that it was any concern of his. To leave
his hiding-place he had to overcome an instinctive
reluctance; the other script, the one of which some
lines could be deciphered in the unknown woman's
eyes, had charmed him to the point of making the
first one seem insipid, and only with great effort
did the actor find he could assume once more the
clownish guise of Sganarelle.

WE CAN ASSUME THAT during the interval Vulpius did not much heed his colleagues' talk, nor perhaps even the curt compliments of the superintendent, who made a fleeting appearance in the dressing-rooms, vanishing at once to resume attendance on his guests. Even the presence of Dora, who moved around him with her cheeks reddened and her eyes sparkling, perhaps failed to erase altogether from his mind the pale figure of the unknown woman.

The young actress seemed in the grip of an uncontainable euphoria, which was due only partly to the warm applause with which the audience, particularly its male members, had accompanied her exit from the stage. She rejoiced most of all in the success of Sganarelle, who had managed to provoke such extraordinary hilarity among the spectators, and she now recalled in detail for her friend's sake the most important phases of that triumphant progress which she herself had witnessed from the wings. Without a doubt the play would end with nothing short of a standing ovation in tribute to him, and when the local critic's article appeared they would see to whom the most lavish praise would go, between Vulpius and that old windbag of a leading actor. Assuming, added Dora, that the distinguished reviewer was up to expressing an objective judgement; he too was an old windbag when it came down to it, and solidarity with his own kind might cloud his judgement. But even in such an unfortunate case, Vulpius should not be discouraged, because the verdict that mattered was that of the public, and she knew with total certainty the object of the public's preferences.

This passionate line of reasoning was brusquely interrupted every time the sound of footsteps echoed outside the dressing-room. Then both of them looked towards the door and paused in anticipation, Dora fearing the entrance of an irate Don Juan who had heard her from the corridor, Vulpius in the hope of receiving a visit from the unknown woman. But the interval ended without anything of the kind occurring; Sganarelle went back on-stage and Dora took her place again in the wings to watch his success and the further humiliation of the leading actor, who in truth had no sense whatsoever of being eclipsed by his colleague and indeed kept up his own role with all the ease of being the public's darling.

Above where Dora stood, to the left, was the opening of the box where the beautiful watcher sat, and neither of the two appeared to have eyes for anyone but Sganarelle. Not even the statue, which arrived punctually for supper at the end of the fourth act, managed to shift their attention from him. Whenever he could, Vulpius returned the looks of now one, then the other, but on Dora his thoughts lingered only fleetingly; that buxom girl with her shadowless light eyes seemed to him almost bereft of charm compared with the woman sitting in the proscenium box. The gloom that hid her from him urged him to fill out the picture all by himself, to give her definite features, to assign her an identity; but none of the conjectures crossing his mind seemed to him to do justice to that aura of adventure and of mystery with which, at least in his eyes, the unknown woman was surrounded. Vulpius savoured this game with a certain advance nostalgia, since he could guess at its fragility, its inevitable conclusion; doubtless after the performance someone would introduce the enigmatic lady to him as the mayor's cousin or the post office chief's sister-in-law; it could not be otherwise in that town where everyone knew everyone else, and no one ended up there without some clear reason. Therefore he might as well resign himself in advance to a commonplace solution to the intrigue which he had sketched out in fantasy. Yet he had most of the fifth act to come, there still was time before reality reasserted its humdrum rights, and meanwhile, why should he deny himself the pleasure of those speculations, of those looks between them, of that mute dialogue?

In recording such thoughts I am afraid of having given the impression that our protagonist was a particularly frivolous individual, and if moreover I were to put forward the suspicion that the presence of the unknowing Dora made the game even more exciting for him, there are some who would judge him downright cruel. But frivolity and cruelty, it can be answered, are privileges of the imagination, and Vulpius nurtured these dangerous passions with a mind untroubled in the sure knowledge of having to discard them at the end of the play, just like his make-up and costume. In his eyes they were not endowed with any greater reality than that which could be assigned to everything on the stage which acquires an ephemeral existence, only to sink again into nothingness as soon as the curtain goes down, without any trace left behind except in the pages of a script.

However, these fantasies occupied only a cranny of his mind, which remained focused above all on the performance. In Don Juan's palace the last flesh-and-blood guest had taken his leave, and any minute now visitors of quite a different sort were expected. During the brief dialogue between master and servant the lights dimmed, creating an atmosphere which was propitious to spectral apparitions, and indeed these were not long in arriving. An ominous drum roll rose up from the orchestra as a female figure wrapped in a white veil advanced hieratically from the back of the stage. She was so thickly swathed that her form could hardly be made out, yet Don Juan seemed to conceive a great interest in her at once, and after casting the audience a look of complicity he hurriedly went towards her; but the woman immediately dampened his enthusiasm by exhorting him to repentance and threatening him with eternal damnation as an alternative. Undaunted, Don Juan took a few steps closer, and the woman let her veil fall; now she displayed all the emblems of transience: her face was a leering death's head, one white hand held a scythe and the other a golden hourglass. When the stubborn sinner made to strike her with his sword, the lights suddenly went out; a moment later they were lit again and the spectre had disappeared.

Without giving either the characters or the audience time to recover from their fright, the stone guest emerged from the wings and held out his hand to Don Juan; the orchestra set about making a din in imitation of crashing thunder and the trapdoor opened wide, a pale representation of the infernal abyss, emanating a reddish vapour which very quickly engulfed the stage and hid both the libertine and the Commendatore. Brightly coloured sparks rose from all sides as in a fireworks display. Sganarelle, who had rushed to the front of the stage to escape that pandemonium, turned his back to the audience to watch his master's well-deserved end. As he stood there, motionless, he saw that the glare also illumined the proscenium box and for an instant he managed to discern the face of the unknown woman; then the smoke cleared, the Catherine wheels stopped exploding, and that face was again swallowed up by the darkness.

Don Juan's screams sounded ever more distant and muffled; when they had ceased altogether,

Sganarelle recalled with consternation that heavenly justice had defrauded him of wages, but the curtain, falling abruptly, cut short his complaints.

THE ACTORS TOOK SEVERAL curtain calls, and it
seemed that the thundering of applause would never
end; only the critic from the local paper confined
himself to a symbolic clapping with a soundless tap
of one hand on the back of the other, yet his smiles
left no doubt that he would write a glowing review.

Vulpius shot a glance at the proscenium box, but
the woman had gone already. At last the actors withdrew to their dressing-rooms, where very soon a
not insignificant section of the audience poured in
after them: those with even a superficial acquaintance with some member of the company, those who
deemed themselves authorised to represent the community by virtue of positions they held, those who
were connected by ties of blood or friendship to
members of either of these categories, did not let
slip the chance to exchange a few words face to face
with those creatures who a short time before had
been so alien and inaccessible, and, with a mixture
of relief and disappointment, see for themselves that

these were perfectly ordinary people, so that the
narrow little rooms behind the stage were transformed into salons through which the
superintendent circled breathlessly with the zeal of
a genuine host.

Many came to Vulpius too to bring congratulations, and every time someone came knocking on
the door he hoped to see his mysterious admirer;
but among the elegant ladies who wandered from
one dressing-room to the other, expressing to all and
sundry their garrulous enthusiasm, there was not
one who even remotely resembled her. After a time,
however, he gave up expecting her; it was a night
for celebration, the company was the centre of attention and general fussing and his own role had to be
kept up in the best possible way, not the role of
Sganarelle any more, but the role of Vulpius, the
young actor who was confident of his talent and yet
ready to hear out other people's suggestions with
due modesty, conducting himself with the utmost
propriety and yet with a faint whiff of the rake
about him, without which a theatrical type would
have been quite unimaginable in the eyes of respectable citizens.

Vulpius was extremely skilful at maintaining the
right balance between the two extremes; he managed
simultaneously to inspire respect and liking, to
charm and to put at ease. On these worldly occasions
his every word, his every gesture, was calibrated
with absolute precision, just as if on-stage, yet he
never showed the slightest trace of sycophancy or
condescension towards anyone, nor did he abandon

his own detached stance. In him, simulation, if one can call it that, was a kind of remoteness, an extreme reserve which was not diminished even when the audience shook his hand in the dressing-room or sat down with him at a restaurant table, instead of applauding him from the stalls.

So if in social relations his actor's temperament was expressed as a predilection for artifice and a complete refusal of spontaneity, the more common affectations of theatrical types were nonetheless alien to him, like gushing talk, for instance, or the custom of greeting anyone in that milieu with hugs and kisses like some close relative. Even with Dora he avoided any effusiveness in public, and she would often tease him about this somewhat haughty aloofness; it was, on the other hand, the object of admiration among the well-bred townswomen, who set much store by his 'gentlemanly ways'.

That night Vulpius's mask seemed even more firmly in place than usual, in striking contrast with the cheerful excitement that prevailed among the other members of the company. Dora, surrounded by a cluster of admirers, gave free rein to a playful flirtatiousness, and when Vulpius passed by the dressing-room crammed with flowers, she gave him an ambiguous look, which was both challenging and complicitous, to which his answer was a faintly ironic smile; sunk in an armchair, the leading actor listened with sly reverence to the celebrated theatre critic, who was describing to him the innermost secrets of his performance, while the bony Doña Elvira, engaged in conversation with the mayor's wife, paraded the whole repertoire of aristocratic manners that she had picked up over years of playing queens and countesses.

To celebrate the opening, a supper had been planned in one of the town's smartest restaurants, an event which the actors viewed with some apprehension, for experience had taught them that on such occasions one eats little and badly; and, indeed, as they sat down at those richly laid-out tables in front of a watery soup or a thin slice of roast meat, almost all of them, although flattered by the attendance of so many influential notables, thought wistfully of the copious dishes served in the boarding-house restaurant.

Before dessert, Vulpius, who had been assigned a place next to the superintendent, endeavoured to draw some information from him about the woman in the box, though without achieving great results. The superintendent was distracted by countless obligations; between one mouthful and the next he had to keep his attention on the intricate web of diplomatic connections which so much contributed to the theatre's prosperity; right now he could do without pandering to the idle curiosity of an actor. And the thing was that he didn't know this lady, he hadn't even seen her. Perhaps Vulpius was unaware that the Municipal Theatre enjoyed the greatest prestige far and wide and its programme could very well attract an audience from outside the area, even foreigners; there had already been instances of this kind in the not-too-distant past. This being so, he really could not understand why so much notice should be taken of the presence of an unknown woman.

Vulpius was not much impressed by this parading of cosmopolitan nonchalance, but all he could do was resign himself; after giving him this brusque response, the superintendent had resumed talking to another supper companion, and the young man embarked upon a dull conversation with a lady sitting opposite him.

It was almost dawn when the supper ended and, still fairly hungry, the actors all made their way together towards the boarding-house. Now that the day was over, demanding as it had been, they felt as if relieved of a heavy burden. As they traversed the silent streets they cast off the impeccable demeanour they had had to maintain with such effort for so long, and they laughed, shouted, exchanged some-what uncharitable comments about the esteemed citizens with whom they had dined, and all in all seemed determined to make up for the constraints they had endured with an outburst of infantile high spirits. Only on Vulpius's face the mask did not slip altogether, even though he was now beside Dora and was walking arm in arm with her. Until that moment he had scarcely remembered her existence, and now he experienced a confused sense of guilt, of which he tried to rid himself through numerous attentions.

But Dora had not even noticed his vagueness, so much was her heart brimming over with the success of the opening, the gallantries of her admirers and the luxurious atmosphere of the restaurant. By contrast, she noticed at once the small signs of affection which Vulpius devoted to her, and with this unaccustomed tenderness it seemed to her that her happiness was complete. She looked around and she drank in the bracing air, thinking back over the details of the evening, and every memory and sensation reverberated back to her with full and flawless sound, as if she had run her nail around a goblet of the purest crystal.

THE PERFORMANCES RAN ON, evening after evening, and each evening Vulpius saw the unknown woman stare at him, only to disappear at the end of the play; even as the bows were taken, when the lights went on again in the hall they revealed only the empty box and the corridor wall behind the open curtain. Then Vulpius took his eyes away from this disappointing sight and withdrew to his dressing-room, where, he was sure by now, the unknown woman would not come to him.

Throughout those days he was so uneasy, so absorbed in his own thoughts, that Dora finally became aware of it. It happened often that when spoken to by her or by a colleague he did not answer or answered only after some time, as if his attention had to re-emerge from who knew what remoteness; at table, too, he was unusually taciturn, and although she did everything to convince herself to the contrary Dora could not manage to banish the suspicion that what drove him into her bedroom at night was nothing more than force of habit.

Perhaps, she mused anxiously, Vulpius was sickening for something, or perhaps he was tormented by some worry he did not want to confide; and yet these peculiarities did not seem to have their origin in unpleasantness; no, she often had the sensation that her friend withheld from her not a grief but some joy. More than once she tried to penetrate this mystery by asking the cards, from which, however, she got only contradictory answers; even the portents offered as always in great abundance by everyday life were indecipherable to her, since they referred simultaneously to contrasting situations, events that were cheerful and gloomy – in other words, instead of clarifying the ambiguity of Vulpius's behaviour they gave of it a faithful representation, from which her simple heart could draw no certainty but only further disquiet.

So if Dora's mood had somewhat altered since the opening night, if anguished doubts increasingly darkened the radiant serenity of her nature, all this escaped Vulpius entirely; the fact was that the girl forced herself in every way to appear happy and carefree as usual, and, although assumed without special skill, this pretence was more than enough to deceive so thoughtless an observer.

Now the young actor would go to the theatre very early, when his colleagues were still lingering in their rooms at the boarding-house, and he would sit for a long time in front of the dressing-room mirror, devoting scrupulous care to his make-up and costume. On their arrival the others would find him quite ready to go on stage, and yet, in an unceasing search for perfection, he continued making small improvements to his appearance, so that every night Sganarelle acquired new features which made his characterisation ever more precise and convincing. Well in advance of the start of the play, he would leave his dressing-room to go on to the set and would stay there, taking no heed of the astonished glances of the scene-changers who bustled around him, and listening to the sounds that came incoherently from the hall. When at last – never soon enough – the curtain was raised and put an end to his impatience, he delivered his lines giving his all, and on edge to the point where he might have been facing rows of demanding critics instead of an easily pleased audience at a repeat performance.

This zeal was in stark contrast to the attitude of his colleagues, who seemed more relaxed with every evening that passed and who after the upheaval of the opening regarded the rest of the run as merely routine and altogether devoid of surprises. Vulpius, however, continued to deepen his performance, demonstrating a tenacity which made the others shake their heads in amusement.

But the audience to which Vulpius consecrated his talent was made up of one single spectator and he was able to apply himself with greater freedom to observing her in the calmer atmosphere of repeat performances. By the second night he could already make out something of her dress, a dark, very low-cut dress which had, nonetheless, the effect of being very severe, perhaps because on the unknown woman's breast there were no jewels to be seen. Her hair, falling straight and smooth like a black veil, partly covered her shoulders, and in the stage lights it glowed with reflections that went from bronze to an icy blue. She held her upper body erect and sometimes, if Vulpius were at the back of the stage, she leaned out slightly towards the balustrade and then drew back as soon as he came closer. But her eyes always followed him, and they held his sudden looks without flinching.

Vulpius was in no doubt that this solitary individual came to every performance solely on his account; why, then, had she never attempted to approach him? After all, visiting an actor in his dressing-room was a perfectly acceptable thing to do. Perhaps, the young man thought, it was shyness that prevented her; and yet a woman who was shy would not have stared at him with such insistence, insolence even, without taking care to conceal her own interest. The more he reflected on this behaviour, the less he was able to explain it to himself, and he did not even have the means to come to any conclusions about the unknown woman's identity. Her attire and the style of her hair, which were so plain, so untouched by any kind of fashion, placed her in a sense outside time, as though she were wearing a simple costume for some totally abstract and stylized performance, throwing her into extraordinary relief in that hall overburdened with ornament.

Yet there was nothing drab about the way she was

dressed. On the contrary, it struck Vulpius with a sumptuous impression, and the very splendour of the theatre was reduced in his eyes to a flimsy outline which, thanks only to the woman sitting in the box, was able to form itself into a clear and significant image. The other women in the audience, on whom occasionally his attention would fleetingly rest, were there as guests; whereas the unknown woman seemed to have her own authentic abode in the theatre, to a degree that made it almost imposs-ible for him to think of her outside it.

This did not subdue in him the desire to see her at close quarters, and to speak to her, but instead this desire grew every day more intense. After the performances he could scarcely tolerate the company of the other actors with their invasive cordiality, and towards Dora, too, he felt a certain annoyance; her beauty appeared to him something flagrant and bereft of mystery, he was irritated by the showy clothes she wore, her sweet tooth for candies and chocolates, the thoughtlessness with which she settled for her own unpolished perform-ances. Yet he took the very greatest care to repress this intolerance, I dare not say whether out of regard for Dora or to exclude her completely from his secret.

Neither she nor anyone else had ever shown any sign of having noticed the unknown woman, and Vulpius considered this situation to be quite natural; what happened between them, that strange blend of intimacy and distance, allowed no witnesses, and in its very essence eluded the gaze of any outsiders.

Dora could not perceive the woman sitting in the box, just as she could not read her companion's most profound thoughts; in either event, had this knowledge of his been contradicted, it would have been a source of wonderment and incredulity. Yet he felt himself obliged to protect both of these so different creatures from each other, letting each of them reign undisturbed in her own sphere.

At night, as soon as Vulpius closed his eyes, the image of the girl who slept beside him would abruptly wane in his memory and that of the unknown woman would rise, pale and lunar, her own inaccessibility preserved even as the object of his fantasies. Vulpius did not dream of meeting her, he merely saw her before him as he had seen her just a few hours before from the stage, and all his faculties focused on this vision with a rigorous fervour that made it increasingly real, and the darkness in which his closed eyes were lost became the darkness of the theatre, and the flickering gleams perceived inside his eyelids were the changing reflections of the stage lights. Then the tension began to slacken and the reflections dimmed, one by one, as Vulpius sank into his motionless sleep.

THE OPAQUE FIGURE, THE newborn character whom we glimpsed at the boarding-house table, seems by now to have acquired a less elusive nature; if we knew almost nothing about him to begin with, we now at least are acquainted with the centre of gravity around which his existence has begun to revolve with a movement which is destined to spin ever faster into obsession. It may be that the sway of this obsession was not so total in reality, that other thoughts too, other desires, continued to occupy his mind, but for us Vulpius is primarily someone who in the course of a performance found himself being observed by an unknown woman in the audience and who ever since then, night after night, has conducted that dialogue of looks to which we have referred. By distilling and simplifying, by highlighting the essential and neglecting the count-less casual details with which life likes to muddle its pattern, in the growing attraction exercised upon him by the woman in the box we can discern a deep fascination, one of those fires that blaze up from a small spark and then spread irresistibly, devouring and obliterating everything they find in their path.

Even in this case I do not mean to assert that Vulpius was in love; if I did so I would be saying too much and too little, and above all I would be telling another story, one which is also possible, but very different from mine. As far as I am concerned, I prefer not to give a name to the feeling which at that time was troubling Vulpius's spirit; if we wished we could designate it with an x and read these pages as an algebraic equation which, if worked out correctly, will produce the value x in the end. I am not inclined, however, to rule out the possibility that this value can be attained only to an approximate degree, nor that there may be more than one term which turns out to equal our unknown factor; if this is so, it would in a sense justify the choice of writing a novel rather than that of the equation, which would have been simpler and more reliable, and less apt to being misunderstood.

For now, let us confine ourselves to our x and say that it eventually imposed itself upon Vulpius to the point where it turned his days into a succession of empty hours of waiting, his evenings into an anxious straining for a satisfaction which was invariably denied him. Meanwhile the run was about to end, with only two or three more performances before the transfer to the second play in the programme, which was already being rehearsed every afternoon between three and six. Vulpius divided himself between Sganarelle and the new character, but he was worried by this imminent change: how could he be sure that when *Don Juan* was replaced by the new production the unknown woman would continue coming to the theatre? Certainly, he was convinced that this woman's attention was directed at him and not the work, and yet he understood too little the reasons for her behaviour to know which convergence of circumstances shaped it, and to what respective degrees.

On the last night, as he responded to the unknown woman's looks from his hiding-place behind the bush, it suddenly crossed his mind to take advantage of the interval to go and meet her in her box or in the foyer. He had always thought he had to wait for the woman to visit him; perhaps it was up to him to join her, introduce himself and find some way of speaking to her. He was in no doubt that once they were face to face their mutual embarrassment would very soon be overcome and everything between them would be natural, not an encounter between strangers but a bringing fully to light of what until now had developed in that furtive and almost unexpressed way.

Therefore as soon as the curtain had fallen he rushed into his dressing-room, took off his hat and Sganarelle's braided jacket, put on his own and hurried out as fast as he could. As he passed by Dora's dressing-room he saw with relief that the girl was absorbed in close conversation with the young actress who played the part of the spectre; he gave her a curt nod and went on. Only when he reached the door leading to the foyer did he realise that he could not enter. He still wore his stage make-up, and apart from the jacket his clothes were more than two centuries out of date; he would certainly not have gone unobserved. So all he did was walk around the foyer along the deserted corridor, peeping warily through, but he failed to catch any glimpse of the one he sought. Then he headed for the proscenium box. On the steps he ran into a group of playgoers who stared at him in bewilderment; he gave them one of Sganarelle's bows executed to perfection and went straight on without looking round.

The curtains closing off the box were still drawn. In the grip of keen excitement Vulpius reached out and parted them a little. All he found were some empty chairs, all of them set against the wall except one which had been pushed forwards to the balustrade.

For a little while he stayed there looking across at the boxes on the other side, at the curtain hiding the stage, which was very near, at the stalls, where only a very few spectators remained in their places leafing through the programme. This, then, was the view presented to the unknown woman when she took her seat and waited for the lights to go down; her eyes too would rest on those stuccoes, on the enormous crystal blooms that hung from the ceiling, on the coat of arms supported by the cupids. For a moment he had an urge to be there when the curtain went up so that he could watch himself exactly as she watched him.

At last he turned to look at the chair; in the middle

of the seat there gleamed a small gold watch. He took it up, holding it delicately between his fingers. On the white oval face the hours were inscribed in black, in Roman numerals, and Vulpius noticed that the hands indicated two o'clock. He brought the watch case to his ear, but could hear no ticking.

When the stalls began to fill up again, he realised that there were only a few minutes to go before the interval ended. He left hurriedly and returned to his dressing-room, where Dora was waiting patiently at her ease on the divan, and only then was he aware that he still had the watch held tightly in his hand. He slipped it quickly into a pocket, then, pretending not to see his girlfriend's questioning look, he changed his jacket, put on his hat and went to the mirror to set his costume in order. Dora peered at him in perplexity, but remarked only that the stage manager had already come in search of him and that they were waiting just for him so that they could start the fourth act. Vulpius asked her to go and let them know that he was ready, and a moment later he was back on stage.

He was so unsettled by this precipitous transition that it was some time before he could concentrate on his part again, but he finally regained his usual confidence. By the second scene, he was able to take advantage of an opportune moment and looked towards the proscenium box; the curtain was half open as he had left it, the dimmed light from the corridor faintly illumined the walls, and there was no one sitting by the balustrade.

IX

IN THE BOARDING-HOUSE restaurant the actors applied themselves to supper with cheerful alacrity. The thick, steaming cream of chicken soup, served in large porcelain cups, was enough to restore them, spoonful by spoonful, after the rigours of performance. The actor-manager, who, at the end of the play had rebuked Vulpius with paternal severity for his flight from the dressing-room during the interval, now seemed pacified and willing to make his contribution to the establishment of universal harmony, and he did no more than shake his head from time to time in the direction of that rash young man.

Dora, too, pretended to have forgotten the incident and to be satisfied with the vague and reticent excuses with which Vulpius countered the leading actor's reproaches. At first she had hoped that when they were able to have a word together in private he would be less sparing of explanations about his strange behaviour, and for this reason as they walked side by side from the theatre to the boarding-house

61

she had slowed down so that they could detach themselves from the rest of their fellow actors. Very soon the two of them were left alone, but he strode on in silence, as if absorbed in solemn thoughts, from which Dora dared not distract him with her questions. The streets, lit only dimly by the yellowish lamplight, seemed to her hostile and inhospitable, and for comfort's sake she had clung more tightly to Vulpius's arm, whereas he had given no sign of noticing this gesture; he seemed to greet his girlfriend's closeness with indifference, looking at her without seeing her, and whenever she tried to strike up a conversation he would give an offhand answer, then take refuge once again in that cold silence of his.

Now, sitting at the table, enlivened by the noisy presence of her fellows, Dora experienced a sense of relief; Vulpius's attitude became less troubling in that brightly lit room where conversations were entwined all around her and the constant stream of dishes created endless diversions. In one way or another he'll get over it, she told herself, and little by little she managed to take heart by drawing on the inexhaustible resources of her fatalism; and yet she could not entirely erase the memory of the dread with which she had been seized when she had leant on Vulpius's arm and felt it as stiff and lifeless as an arm made of wood.

The roast was some time in coming, and that delay made the actors keenly impatient. Each time a waiter set foot in the room every face was turned towards him, either in indignation or in supplication, depending on respective temperaments, but in every case animated by the conviction that their common lot was a matter of his good offices with the cook. Alone, Vulpius did not even look up when this happened; he kept staring straight ahead, as if he saw some particularly fascinating spectacle in the glasses of wine which crowded the centre of the table, and his thoughts kept revolving around the unknown woman. It astonished him that she had quit the theatre at the end of the third act, and he feared that this action was a consequence of the reckless step he had taken. Perhaps it had been madness, had been an intrusion, to try so brutally to violate the reserve in which this woman liked to be enclosed, to cross the boundary in a single leap. If he never saw her again, he would have only himself to thank.

And yet, the more he thought it over, the more it seemed to him that something contradicted this interpretation. He slipped his hand into the pocket where he had put the watch and his fingers lightly touched the fine-linked wristband, the smooth glass of the face. This jewel left so blatantly in the middle of the seat had perhaps not been forgotten but set there deliberately for him to find it; perhaps it was a pledge, a sign, containing some message to be deciphered. The hands stopped at two o'clock came to mind again, and suddenly there was born in him the conviction that the unknown woman had wished to make an assignation with him. Of course, that must be it; in this light everything was clear. And if the time was thereby fixed unequivocally, there could also be only one meeting-place.

He jumped to his feet, attracting the notice of his colleagues. They must excuse him: he had realised he had left something in his dressing-room. No, he could not put it off till tomorrow, and nor was there any point in Dora taking the trouble to go with him. But would the actor-manager be so kind as to lend him his key?

As soon as he had it he rushed out of the restaurant. He was halfway there when he heard the church bells chime twice, and he quickened his step so as not to arrive too late. Overcome as he was with excitement, he would certainly have got lost if the road had been less familiar, but even though he hardly looked where he was going, he always managed to take the right turning, guided by the same instinct which governs the unconscious advance of sleepwalkers.

The theatre square was deserted, heavy wooden shutters locked the three great arched doors like lowered eyelids, and the building, usually so welcoming, seemed stubbornly self-contained. Vulpius reached the stage door, and saw no one here either. He waited for some minutes, then it occurred to him that perhaps the unknown woman wanted to meet him not in the street but inside the theatre; so, using the key, he went in, and left the door ajar.

As he groped his way in the dark it took him some time to find the electrical switches. When the lights finally went on, he headed down the corridor and noticed the two big communal dressing-rooms used by the extras which opened out either side. Empty like this they gave an impression of bleakness, and only the objects left scattered about by the actors – costumes and jars of cosmetics, unlikely talismans and the crumpled pages of scripts – attenuated the sense of dereliction. Dora's dressing-room was also open; a large brass crucifix hung above the mirror and the flowers that had been sent on the opening night quietly rotted in their vases. Vulpius felt inexplicably embarrassed, as if he had intruded on someone's privacy, and he hurriedly closed the door.

The big clock on the wall showed it was ten past two. Vulpius went back along the corridor as far as the exit and looked out, but there was not a living soul to be seen in the street. He returned inside, worried by this delay, and to take his mind off it he resumed his wandering through the dressing-rooms, looking closely at the costumes which hung along the walls, some of them limp and shapeless, others stiff as empty hulls. Here Don Alonso's plumed hat lay atop the sumptuous folds of a cloak, there the austere starched ancient Roman's tunic which was given an airing on stage by the Commendatore's statue shared a hanger with a threadbare black silk kimono covered in gold dragons. In the women's dressing-room, the scythe and hourglass with which the spectre had tried to inspire a terror of death and damnation in the libertine were set out on a table top in the guise of elegant knick-knacks. Vulpius went over, turned the hourglass upside down and stood looking at the sand that fell through the narrow neck, but at once all interest in the object and its pedantic symbolism went out of his mind;

he fancied he heard a sound in the corridor, perhaps the rustling of a woman's clothes. In an instant he reached the dressing-room threshold. He saw the deserted corridor, yet could not persuade himself that he was mistaken. He thought the unknown woman had gone in advance of him in the direction of the hall, that she wanted to await him there, possibly in the proscenium box, and he in turn made his way, but not in that direction; he now believed he knew exactly how their meeting would take place. After pressing all the switches, he therefore went up on to the stage, where the concave surface of the backdrop, untransfigured by the play of lights, was revealed as a mere piece of fabric of imprecise hue, and with all his strength he pulled on the curtain cable.

The heavy pall of velvet ascended to disclose first the stalls, then the diverse ranks of boxes and balconies. There was no one in the proscenium box, and in vain did Vulpius's eyes scour every corner of the hall. He was making quite sure more than anything else, since from the start he had been sure he was in an empty theatre. Suddenly a shiver ran through him; only now did he notice that this place was extraordinarily cold. And yet something detained him, an intense, almost morbid curiosity, which gradually possessed him to the point of making him forget why he had come.

He stood at the front of the stage, still scanning the hall. The little twisted columns, the broad draperies of the curtains, the friezes of flowers that wound along the balconies, all had a totally new aspect, so much did Vulpius have the impression of seeing them for the first time; the sumptuousness of the theatre, undisturbed by any human presence, displayed itself with such potency that it aroused a peculiar sense of awe in the young man, almost as if he had stumbled upon a sacred place, and at the same time it seemed to him that the slight but persistent iciness, of which he still was aware, emanated just from that gilt, from those velvets and decorations.

In this protective and well-trodden hall, where the actors felt at home and the audience was made as welcome as in the dwelling of some solicitous Amphitryon, there was now nothing welcoming, nothing familiar, and, perturbed, Vulpius wondered why. Perhaps it is the silence, he thought, such a deep silence in which every single thing assumes a different significance, removed from all the bonds of habit to become locked in its own infinitely strange, infinitely hostile essence. And he was amazed that he had never had the least inkling of this essence, that he had performed there for years, night after night, without what surrounded him ever prompting the slightest unease.

In the unbridled exuberance of ornaments he had never discerned that undertone which now appalled him and held him fast, and to which he was yet unable to give a name; he had an obscure sense that the gildings and statues, columns and chandeliers, were intent upon both hiding and revealing something, and he strove to understand the nature of this something, like a person trying to guess the extremely simple word that forms the key to a complicated cipher.

He went down into the stalls, and when he had got to one of the back rows he sat and examined the empty stage, harshly lit by the house lights, which produced a striking contrast with the fullness of shapes and colours shown off in the hall. It seemed to him quite incredible that this nothingness should give rise to everything, to such a multiplicity of places and landscapes, characters and destinies, a phantasmagoria which could mask it for a few hours and give an appearance of life to the rigid splendour which enveloped it. And yet, what could be the source of the spell exercised by this appearance, if not the nothingness which was its secret background? The painted drapes, the costumes, the words and gestures delivered on the stage, in all of this Vulpius at once discerned a series of allusions to this background, to this premise which was never expressed nor represented but which showed itself to him for the first time tonight with perfect clarity.

He went back on stage and turned out all the lights, leaving lit only the crystal clusters which hung from the columns. Now the boxes were plunged in a soft and yielding penumbra in which Vulpius's imagination could freely give form to its own figures, for the most part watching women with long dark hair and black eyes fixed upon him. The stage was a great dark rectangle, an opaque night ignorant of moon and stars, but Vulpius turned on a spotlight and aimed its beam upon the backdrop to transform it into a dazzling surface. He turned

out the lights in the hall and changed the filters, and
one after the other all the colours of the rainbow
shone over the stage; then he turned the spotlight
on the stalls to illuminate now this or that detail. The
columns, the drapes, the caryatids that supported the
boxes, were now the protagonists in a silent drama,
a motionless dumbshow. Each emerged in turn from
the darkness and was swallowed up by the darkness
again as soon as the spotlight's beam moved on;
thus, appearing and disappearing, in their way too
they simulated life, or rather a bizarre variant upon
it, inert, petrified, perpetually absorbed in the repetition of a single gesture, and in that small inanimate
world it seemed to Vulpius that he carried out the
office of a divinity to whom were entrusted creation
and annihilation.

Yet he did not feel so much an author as an
accomplice or a minister to that seductive game
played out by light and shadow within the empty
theatre, and he thought that during performances
too his will, his talent and his very body were only
the partly unconscious means through which a dialogue of this kind was conducted between powerful
agencies. In him, in his person, light and shadow
met, in him they set up understandings, perhaps
found secret affinities, and something of this kind
applied to the lines which he uttered and which, he
knew now, did not erase the silence, but measured
its depth and no more, like plummets dropped down
into an abyss.

Almost without realising it, he had stopped
waiting for the unknown woman. It was nearly four

when he remembered and he understood that she would never come now; reluctantly he decided to go home. As he advanced towards the exit along the dressing-room corridor his disappointment at the missed rendezvous rose up again, but was immediately drowned by a different feeling, by a kind of intoxication which he himself could not entirely explain.

He walked all the way to the boarding-house without the image of the theatre becoming any less vivid or imperious; the streets and the squares, with their dark corners and others where the night illumination bestowed a stage-like emphasis, were its natural prolongation, and in travelling this road Vulpius perceived a charm which he had never discerned before.

When he got to the boarding-house he found the outside door locked, yet he did not ring the bell. At this hour the porter was already asleep, but he knew the hiding-place where in such cases a key was left for late-coming guests. Fortunately, that night too this precaution had been observed, so that a moment or two later Vulpius was climbing the stairs with silent footfalls. He reached the third floor, and still careful not to make a sound he turned into the corridor. When he passed Dora's room he saw a sliver of light leaking under the door. He had a moment's hesitation, then went on towards his own bedroom.

THE DESCRIPTION OF THAT night in the deserted
theatre, when Vulpius's mind was struck by
intuitions, thoughts and images of such importance
in the unfolding of his story, is something I should
like to follow with a crowd scene, so as to hide our
protagonist in the variegated multitude of surrounding characters. It would be even better to
speed up the narration by passing over the days and
the weeks, replacing the precision of the perfect
tense with the recapitulatory fuzziness of the imperfect tense; thus I would achieve the by-no-means-
negligible result of throwing the preceding pages
into relief by making a clean break, and the meaning,
the value, of the events just recounted could mature
undisturbed for both Vulpius and the reader by
removal from the over-harsh light of explicit
attention.

Alas, it is not permissible for me to resort to a
solution of this kind; if I were now to enter into
the doubtful haze of the imperfect, I should leave

unanswered a series of questions which I judge it my duty, however, to answer without unreasonable delay, above all questions about the beautiful unknown woman. A lady whom at this moment I confess I should have liked to see vanish with elegant discretion, on tiptoe, so to speak, without having to expend any further words on the subject.

She did, in fact, vanish, or at any rate she appeared no more in the theatre after the evening when she left the watch on her chair; but the stage exit of such characters is never discreet – indeed, it can even produce a devastating effect on others akin to an atmospheric disturbance; and perhaps Vulpius experienced something not unlike this when the curtain went up the following night and he saw the unknown woman's box occupied by a plump middle-aged couple. We must believe that he was upset by this, deeply upset, although his performance allowed none of his turmoil to show. Only an especially attentive observer could have remarked a few less-than-benevolent glances directed at the two rotund spectators sitting in the proscenium box, and received by them without their turning a hair, in the surmise that these looks were part and parcel of the acting.

Nor can we dispense with returning to the gold watch, at the very least in order to exonerate Vulpius from any accusation of too casually seizing other people's property. Far from harbouring such an intention, the young man had taken the watch with him to the theatre, in the hope of restoring it personally to its rightful owner. Moreover, it would have been an excellent pretext for approaching her, possibly during the interval, and if the stage manager or the actor-manager had asked him again to explain his absence or had surprised him as he was leaving the dressing-room, he would have had a perfectly good and credible ready-made script, whereby he could have enjoyed a rare opportunity to lie while hardly deviating from the true facts; yes, it was his intention to go off again; he had no problem in acknowledging that. To go where? To look for someone. Which someone? An acquaintance who had been to see him in his dressing-room and had left her watch behind there, this watch. Had they really not seen her? Odd, very odd, although in fact she had only stopped by for a few minutes. And besides, with so many comings and goings it could easily happen that a person went unnoticed.

In rehearsing this script to himself, Vulpius had not failed to realise that it would not be easy for him to explain convincingly why he had not entrusted the forgotten piece of jewellery to an usher, or how he imagined he could wander about among the public dressed like that without putting people out a great deal. He was still musing over how he could surmount such obstacles when he was called on stage and the raising of the curtain revealed to him the futility of his daring plan. The watch therefore remained in his jacket pocket, and for several nights it made the walk with Vulpius from the boarding-house to the theatre and from the theatre to the boarding-house; but the proscenium box continued to be either empty or profaned by

✤ PAOLA CAPRIOLO ✤

some irritating presence, so that the young actor was finally persuaded the unknown woman would not return again and he placed that tangible souvenir of his disappointment in a drawer.

Meanwhile, although he was almost entirely taken up with concerns of quite another kind, he could not but notice that Dora exhibited a resentful coldness in relation to him. She had heard him that night going past her bedroom without coming in, and after locking the door she had gone to bed. The anxiety with which she had awaited her friend's return had given way to the torments of mortification which Dora had sleeplessly persisted in inflicting upon herself with a blind fury until dawn. For the first time in her life, perhaps, she seemed to seek out suffering instead of fleeing it, as she deliberately magnified the seriousness of what had happened, driving herself on with the refined cruelty of an expert torturer. In a certain sense this was all a substitute in her eyes for the presence of the young sweetheart who so inexplicably, and before that night, had grown away from her; it brought him closer, made him almost perceptible, as a persecuting spirit which took pleasure in frightening her by appearing here and there in the darkness of the room.

Thus, in her own way, Dora spent that night too with Vulpius, and in the morning, when she at last roused herself from her dark, drowsing fantasies and impelled herself firmly to sit up in bed, it seemed she was pushing away her unworthy lover. If he doesn't want me he's not worth it, she said out loud, giving each syllable emphasis, as if there were someone in the room who could hear her. As soon as she got up she rushed to open the curtains, and the light dissipated the last traces of that wallowing in misery to which she had so dangerously yielded in the night. With an impatience that would have prompted some suspicion in a mind more inclined to introspection, she waited for Vulpius to come and knock on her door; she would call out 'Come in,' she would submit to his kiss while making quite sure not to return it, she would treat him with the haughty imperturbability of a queen granting a brief audience to a somewhat undeserving subject. No mention of the missed night visit, of course, no questions, no recriminations; and if Vulpius tried to justify himself, he would be met with a sceptical, detached attitude, which would show him on the one hand how unwilling she was to accept the validity of his excuses, and on the other how little she cared about the whole business.

She turned the key in the lock, for she thought it undignified to go and open the door to him herself, then sat down at the dressing-table. After nicely arranging the folds in her dressing-gown (not that blue one trimmed with ostrich feathers, but another more severe one, very like the peplum of a tragic heroine), she set about a vigorous brushing of her wavy blond hair. If he doesn't want me he's not worth it, she reiterated with greater conviction as she inspected her own reflection in the mirror.

It would be hard to come up with any objection to the line of conduct Dora had decided on. The only flaw in the strategy arose from the circumstance that, belying all expectation, Vulpius did not come and knock on his girlfriend's door, so that she had to resign herself to keeping in reserve the little drama so precisely worked out in advance until the much less appropriate setting of the dining-room. There her silences and her proud indifference would not make so pronounced an impression, and would be largely obscured by convivial chit-chat; on the other hand, the thought of not meeting Vulpius alone gave Dora ample reassurance that she would not yield.

She dressed unhurriedly and went down to the restaurant a little late, so as to make her entrance when all the others were already gathered round the table. Catching sight of Vulpius, she felt a sudden tremor between her throat and her breast, but she did not falter and as she made her way to her place she bestowed upon the whole company, except for the young actor, the most radiant of smiles.

Sitting down across from Vulpius, she answered his greeting with a vague nod which would have incurred the envy of the aristocratic Doña Elvira. Then, throughout the whole meal, she favoured him with no further look or word; instead, with strict impartiality, she divided her attention between the rich dishes served by the waiter and her neighbour on the left, greatly regretting that the latter was not some good-looking man in the prime of life, but the stalwart old actor who took the role of the Commendatore in *Don Juan*, and who seemed by far to prefer to her company that of a bulging glass of red wine, emptied and refilled with scrupulous regularity. He was really not the most suitable person for introducing jealous fury into Vulpius's mind, and at any rate Dora very soon realised that the young man was showing very little interest in what was happening across the table. If she feigned indifference, Vulpius had no need to feign it; each time she cast a furtive glance in his direction, Dora found him absorbed as if brooding over something, and his expression would alter in a way unconnected to what was going on around him; one minute it was solemn, the next peculiarly ecstatic, one minute his brow would be corrugated with deep furrows, the next it would unexpectedly clear, and Vulpius would turn a quick intense smile not at Dora, nor at any of his companions, but at some point in the void between one chair and another, as if the very image of happiness had materialised before his eyes just there.

In short, Dora had no success of any kind in calling Vulpius's attention to her act as an outraged queen. Dejected and perplexed, after lunch she withdrew to her room, where she spent the rest of the afternoon trying to drown her sorrows by bingeing on the contents of the comfort cupboard. She would not go to the rehearsal, she did not feel like it, and besides it was not even worth putting herself out for the sake of those two throwaway lines that she had in the new play. She was indisposed, and had every right to be so; and at least Vulpius was bound to notice her absence.

He did indeed notice it, and when the rehearsal was over he finally came and knocked to ask, with cold and courteous solicitude, after the state of his girlfriend's health. Swathed in her peplum, she gave him her answer with the same courtesy, the same coldness; it was just a passing malaise, getting better already. It was very kind of him to take the trouble of enquiring, but now he must excuse her, she had other things to do and could not ask him in. Rather than insist, Vulpius withdrew before the girl could have the satisfaction of closing the door in his face.

Obviously Dora's histrionic capacities left something to be desired in life too, because Vulpius went back to his own room without the slightest suspicion that those brusque manners concealed anything other than a faint ill-humour due to indisposition. Only that night, during the performance, when he learned that Dora had left the theatre immediately after her final scene, did he guess at the truth with a fleeting sense of remorse. She had not come to say hello, she had sent him no message, and it occurred to him then that throughout the day she had behaved very strangely; the missed visit the night before must have offended her, it had to be remedied with some word of apology, some sign of affection. But no sooner had such notions taken shape than he pushed them to the back of his mind, regarding this as a matter of no account which he could deal with quite easily some time later; for now a different worry beset him, the sudden disappearance of the unknown woman, and compared with such an event misunderstandings with his blond companion were only tiny specks of dust. He would only have to give one puff to scatter them, today, or tomorrow, or whenever the occasion arose.

When he got back to the hotel he headed automatically for Dora's room, and smiled when he found the door locked. At once he let go of the handle and went off without knocking; after all, he thought, he might as well allow her this childish feud of hers. Tomorrow, or the day after, or whenever the occasion arose, he would set about smoothing out the little contretemps.

XI

I REALISE THAT WHAT was related in the previous chapter does no honour either to Vulpius's perspicacity or to the delicacy of his feelings for Dora. He had acted towards her with clumsy disregard, and now when at last he became aware of having wounded her he did not even seem too eager to remedy it. By way of justification I can only say that on that day and the days that followed he was engaged upon a radical metamorphosis, which almost entirely absorbed his faculties, leaving him very little room for any other consideration. Ever since the image of the unknown woman had led him to the empty theatre plunged in silence, ever since, following in her footsteps, he had penetrated that secret world of light and shadow, of ephemeral epiphanies and abrupt annihilations, Vulpius had ascribed to his own profession a nobility, even a solemnity, which completely altered its essence and its meaning. The monotony and inherent repetition of the actor's craft no longer made it a mediocre routine, but the sign of belonging to a more elevated sphere where everything took place with the iron necessity of a ritual. Entrances and exits, passing from the shadow to the light and from light into shadow: this and nothing but this was the content of the ritual, and yet around it there unfurled a hieratic opulence of sets and costumes, a dazzling effulgence of words, as if that were the very simple centre where all the world's splendour should converge. Entrances and exits, and around this always identical movement the choreographic wisdom of fiction, capable of infinitely varying its forms.

The thought of being himself among those who officiated at that ritual inspired a new pride in him. Just like an initiate, he had given up his profane name to take on another under which it was granted to him to celebrate the variegated mysteries of the stage, but only now, he felt, did those mysteries begin to show him their true nature, and his initiation was on the road to its fulfilment. The obliviously self-satisfied spectators who massed on the far side of the boundary delimiting the esoteric space of illusion seemed to him with each day that passed more colourless, their presence increasingly irrelevant; now, even when the theatre was crowded, Vulpius spoke his lines to empty rows of seats, to the empty hall which that night with such potency had imposed its own reality upon him, or perhaps, as a solitary gladiator, he challenged himself for the entertainment of the invisible woman who still watched him from the terraces of the arena.

Nor did he maintain the least complicity with the

other actors any longer. He behaved as if on stage with him there were no men or women, but only unknowing marionettes among whom he moved with the superior feelings of one who has learned to pull his own strings; and truly he was learning to manipulate himself as if from the outside, to be both puppet and puppeteer, ventriloquist and doll, to treat his own body like some dead thing. The naturalism and self-identification which had marked his manner of delivery were giving way to a new style, a style that was more abstract, with a marked tendency to irony, to fragmentation, to a conscious display of artifice, before which the inexpert and the cognoscenti among the spectators were seen to be equally disoriented.

When he came on stage he still underwent the prodigious transformation that was so much appreciated by the audience, becoming Pilades or Iago, Puck or Harlequin, but it was always as if he held the mask slightly aside to allow a glimpse of the face it covered. And this face – here was the most disconcerting aspect – could not at once be identified with the face of young Vulpius, the one everyone knew, the one who smiled at whoever came to his dressing-room or bowed with aplomb over a lady's hand. He was the same, yet he was not; not even the most cultivated and sophisticated of the cognoscenti could have spelled out what lay behind such an impression, of almost reciprocal estrangement, distinctly separating Vulpius as a person from Vulpius as an actor. It seemed a paradox, indisputably, but every night each one of them, for the modest price of a ticket, was able to touch at close quarters the truth of that paradox. Despite their mobility, despite their enormous range of expressions, the lineaments of Vulpius the actor appeared harder and more rigid than those of Vulpius the person, and at the same time less defined, for under the stage lights they lost many of their individual characteristics and faded into a blurred neutrality; a situation which partly strengthened the not over-reassuring sensation of being in the presence of an artificial being.

This predilection for artifice was, however, one of the points where the two Vulpiuses obviously held perfectly identical views. A detached formality and a certain lack of directness had always characterised his demeanour, but now these modes of behaviour had become so emphatic, and bordered so much on the scornfully haughty, that not even the most well-disposed of the ladies remained inclined to praise them as 'gentlemanly manners'. It was the slow contagion of the new style of acting, a style which charmed the audience with almost hypnotic violence and yet made them regret the good old days when they could still laugh and be moved watching Vulpius's performance without simultaneously being aware of something akin to the grip of an icy hand round the heart.

So, in order to avoid having also the echo of that iciness, the playgoers seldom set foot in his dressing-room any more, and if they really could not manage to keep away they stayed as short a time as possible. Moreover they had a well-founded suspicion that

their visits were not welcome, and that the moment
of leave-taking was greeted by both parties with
the same relief. Around Vulpius's dressing-room,
therefore, there was created in the end an atmosphere of embarrassment, even of mistrust, and the
silence that issued from it had an effect that was all
the more strange in the cordial hubbub that surrounded it.

There, in that small room whose closed door
almost everyone passed without knocking, Vulpius
took off his costume as he would sacred vestments
and hung it up with extreme care. Sometimes he
liked to recompose its elements, reconstruct upon
the hanger the character he had just played on the
stage; he would spend a long time looking at this
personage who had been suddenly emptied of his
substance, and seemed to see himself in a cruel and
miraculous mirror which was able to strip the flesh
from appearance and lead it back to the nothingness
whence it had come. At other times he would spread
these components along the walls, the coat here, the
leggings there, on the other side the wig or the hat,
shoes and gloves precisely separated, each thing on
its own, like the fragments of a body dismembered
by an explosion. He played these games with great
seriousness, devoting to the methodical demolition
of his character the same passionate zeal with which
every night, before the performance, he brought it
forth anew. Making up and taking make-up off,
dressing and undressing, these habitual procedures
were now the resonating chimes that marked his life,
chimes for which he listened out with ever more

obsessive attention, as if to decipher their secret rhythm.

It was the same rhythm he had discerned that night, when the gilded creatures which populated the empty theatre had revealed themselves to him one after the other beneath the spotlight's beam, but now he seemed always to hear its rising, falling beat, to hear it everywhere, on the stage and in the boarding-house restaurant, in his dressing-room and in the bedroom where he tried to lose himself in sleep. The streets of the town were pervaded by that rhythm which gave sense and coherence to the bustle of the quotidian, which transformed the countless farces of failure into countless variants on a single tragedy, which removed all solidity from the buildings in order to bestow on them the melancholic flimsiness of painted backdrops. That rhythm reverberated from the heavy bronze bells of the church and the many others that answered them in an intertwining dialogue between one tower and the next, ever more distinct as the night went on and sounds subsided, allowing the immemorial purity of those voices to emerge. Often, listening to them from his bed, Vulpius thought that he would have liked to live in those remote times when the city was contained within the ring of bastions like the theatre within its walls, and in the silence the watchkeepers of the night would wander through the streets proclaiming the passing of the hours in words which never varied.

XII

MEANWHILE THE SEASON – in both senses of the word – wore on; dramas and comedies alternated on the stage for the delight of the public, and from her windows Dora no longer saw splashes of green in the city parks, but bare patches of ground on which the trees rose naked and chilled. To get to the theatre she already had to wrap herself up in her overcoat, which that year too had luckily survived the summer assault of the moths and was graced with a new fur collar which framed her face attractively. More and more often, on the way back she would find the town sunk in a fog which was transformed by the lamplight into a peculiar luminous haze where streets and squares, fountains and monuments, dissolved their outlines and changed into bizarre and fantastical creatures. In her opinion weather like this favoured appearances by ghosts, whom no one in any case could have easily distinguished from flesh-and-blood people; for this reason Dora was glad not to have to make the nocturnal trip back to the boarding-house alone, to sense around her the presence of her colleagues, and above all to have always by her side that handsome dark-haired young man who undoubtedly could protect her from any earthly or unearthly danger.

The reconciliation between the two had taken place some time before; at the first words of affection uttered by Vulpius, Dora had set aside her resentment and the following night, in her bedroom, the settling of their little quarrel had been duly celebrated with a bottle of sparkling wine. Everything seemed then to be back to normal, at least so far as the relationship between them was concerned. Certainly, not even the trusting Dora could conceal from herself that Vulpius's behaviour appeared somewhat odd; she was a little worried, for instance, by his new love of solitude; and also that ecstatic concentration she had perceived in him at the time of *Don Juan* seemed still to grip him, making him sometimes blind and deaf to everything around him.

Thank heavens, however, Dora's willing mind had contrived an explanation for all this: Vulpius, as she had always known, was destined to become a very great actor, one of those brilliant personages whose names sooner or later would be known worldwide and would be handed down to posterity with reverence. But the maturation of genius, she had even read somewhere, is never trouble-free, and what was happening now could be understood as the stirring of the chrysalis within the cocoon that still imprisoned it. As soon as this container was broken, as soon as the butterfly had begun to unfurl all the brilliance of its colours, she would be repaid with interest for the sorrows suffered in that transitional phase. Once he became a great man, Vulpius would thereby become a totally happy man, and his happiness would be reflected upon whoever lived beside him, upon whoever had always encouraged him with her affection, supported him with her patience. This was why, whenever her fellow actresses cast her glances of commiseration for some eccentricity Vulpius displayed, Dora would smile with the pride demonstrated to the ignorant by one who knows herself privy to a precious secret.

What is more, that Vulpius's thoughts at this time were devoted almost entirely to the theatre was something confirmed for her by a singular occurrence: for some time now, whenever Dora was onstage without him Vulpius had stayed and watched her from the wings, something he had never done before, and he watched her with such attention, with such intensity, that often when the girl chanced to meet his eyes she felt captured by them, and the prompter had to intervene to remind her of her lines. After the performance he gave her no compliments on her acting, and Dora was not surprised at this; on the contrary, she found it natural that her own modest talent should seem of no account to the future great actor; and yet she had almost the impression of being of more interest to him on the stage than off it, and that only in those moments did he really see her. If instead of her costume she was wearing everyday clothes, and even if she displayed herself to him in one of her seductive negligees, Vulpius's eyes would merely flit past her distractedly, as if she were some over-familiar image; then to forgive him she had to think of the cares of genius, the restless chrysalis, or make a conscious effort to let herself be beguiled by his nice, solicitous ways.

For, ever since the day of their reconciliation, Vulpius had shown his friend a kindness that was boundless, although not without that trace of artifice, that hint of simulation, which had gradually alienated the sympathies of the audience. There were times when he was even tender and passionate, showering her with flowery, amorous words which Dora, fleetingly mistrustful, remembered she had already heard somewhere. Were not these the words, she thought, re-emerging of a sudden from the torpid sentimental intoxication that on such occasions seized hold of her, that perhaps were spoken by Leander to Hero, by Romeo to his Juliet? Despite the unconditional esteem in which she held Vulpius, she could not believe that these were words of his own, and then the tone in which he uttered them, almost declaiming, with that powerful stage whisper which some actors managed to carry as far as the very back rows . . . But in the end what did all this matter? If Vulpius had recourse to the resources that dramatic art put at his disposal to express his own feelings, he was only making use of what belonged to him legitimately, and she had no reason to be offended. Besides, was there not perhaps the shadow of a smile on his face, a subdued irony, as if he did not doubt Dora's capacity to recognise the source of those phrases, while asking her to be his accomplice in a game of courtship? And Dora consented, happy to be able to banish any doubt in order to give herself up unhindered to the harmonious flow of Vulpius's eloquence.

These private playlets were enacted for the most part in his bedroom: it was very seldom and reluctantly that he let himself be induced to leave it to go to Dora's, so that the girl had got into the habit of joining him after supper in that dismayingly stark and tidy room, and sometimes spent the whole night there.

It happened one night that Dora got up and opened a drawer in the chest. I do not know what she was looking for, perhaps a handkerchief or a headache pill, but she forgot about it almost instantly; groping among papers and odds and ends, her fingers had encountered a fine-linked metallic object which her curiosity made her eager to unearth. It was a lovely gold watch, and the young actress inspected it with covetous admiration, while its presence in that bedroom could not but arouse her suspicions.

She went over to Vulpius and showed it to him. 'It's a woman's watch,' she said in an inquisitorial tone as she keenly watched her friend's face, on which, however, there remained unetched the expression of the guilty man caught in the act. His voice too, when he answered her, was calm and unembarrassed. Of course it was a woman's watch, and Dora could have it if she liked it; he would be very pleased to give it to her as a present, especially since her birthday was hardly a week away. 'Then,' said Dora, relieved, 'you bought it for me.' Vulpius preferred not to commit himself to a precise confirmation: 'If you like it,' he merely repeated, 'I'll gladly make you a present of it.'

Delighted with this gift, Dora bent down and gave him a kiss, then fastened the watch on her wrist and lifted her arm to get a better look at her new piece of jewellery. The oval face and the gold band of the bracelet caught the light of the bedside lamp in a myriad sparkling reflections. It was so lovely that Dora could not help bending over Vulpius again and thanking him with another kiss. She went on like this for some time, dividing her tumultuous attention between the gift and the giver; finally, however, it occurred to her that a watch should also show the time, and she noted the position of the hands. 'Is it two o'clock?' she asked Vulpius. 'No, half past two,' he answered after glancing quickly at the pendulum-clock. Then, with the tip of her long, varnished nails, Dora released the winder and moved the hands forward: but as soon as she had done this she perceived that they did not stay in this position, and with every movement of her wrist they slipped on the watchface, as if the pin holding them in place had suddenly come loose.

'Is there something wrong?' enquired Vulpius, seeing her bewilderment. Dora held out her hand to him, showing him the watchface where the hands kept going crazily round and round. He looked at them in silence, then, with an effort, told her that it seemed peculiar and suggested that she try and wind up the watch. But the winder too went round to no avail, and there was no ticking sound from the watchcase. 'Really peculiar,' said Vulpius again, and holding Dora's hand in his he resumed staring at the watchface. He seemed to have forgotten about her completely; the pressure of his fingers became stronger and stronger. 'You're hurting me,' Dora complained, but when she realised that he was not listening to her she freed her hand from his grip with a gesture of impatience.

'What a lovely present,' she said crossly. 'What do you think I'm supposed to do with a watch that doesn't tell the time?' Receiving no answer, she slipped it off and went and threw it back in the drawer.

Only then, when he heard the drawer bang brusquely shut, did Vulpius seem to rouse himself. He assured Dora that he was sorry and that he would bring her another present. She shrugged. She looked at her left hand, which Vulpius's fingers had scored with red marks, and without knowing why she felt a shudder run through her.

 XIII

BUT LET US LEAVE the week between the watch episode and Dora's birthday to go by. Even without going into the details, I can state with reasonable certainty that it does not offer any new departure: the undisturbed sequence of rehearsals, the gatherings round the restaurant table, the comings and goings between the boarding-house and the theatre, everything keeps running with the precision of a well-oiled mechanism, and even Vulpius's eccentricities by now disturb no one, since the municipal actors have managed to neutralise them by ascribing them to the benign category of routine phenomena.

Yet in the limpid rolling back of these days we might catch a dim shadow were we to focus our attention upon Dora again and try to decipher the thoughts that crowded her mind. Confused thoughts, it is true, perhaps not even worthy of the name; they were rather intuitions, anxious forebodings, in short, of the perception that something in the mechanism had broken down, some minute cog, some tiny little wheel, which was almost invisible and yet enough to bring about a faint grating sound which, once it had entered the ear, would no longer leave it. Dora had noticed this unmistakably that evening, when Vulpius, as if mesmerised, had kept staring at the watchface, holding her wrist in a tight, painful grip, and ever since then she had gone on noticing it in each attitude, in each word, in each facet of their relationship.

It troubled her, for instance, that while they were together he would sometimes ask her to repeat just for him some gesture she had enacted on stage, it troubled her that he would take up position in the wings and that often, before and after the performance, he would follow her into her dressing-room, and, with a strange, cold curiosity, watch her as she put on or took off her make-up, as she dressed or shed her costume. Of course, Vulpius had presented all this to her as a game, announcing that he wanted to avail himself of his right to witness the metamorphosis of his very own nymph; but behind the game Dora sensed a hidden seriousness which she could not even begin to comprehend.

Until very recently, whenever they were in the midst of the others she had always been impatient to be left alone with Vulpius, whereas now she would put off that moment for as long as possible, lingering until late talking with her fellow actors. Yet this did not make her less affectionate towards him, indeed, despite the inexplicable fear he inspired in her she would not have given him up for anything in the world. Moreover, she was now particularly assiduous in her dedicated observation and interpretation of the portents, and these were unanimous in heralding the imminence of some extremely important event, some real turning-point which would radically alter her life; she therefore had to be patient until destiny decided to turn the cards face up, and in the meantime try perhaps to propitiate it with suitable spells and supplications. As we know, Dora was an expert in this kind of activity, which if nothing else served to attenuate the sense of powerlessness with which she was sometimes overwhelmed.

The approach of her birthday gave her the certainty of having entered the period that was most favourable to her; the sun and the moon, the planets and the constellations, the entire firmament, were now on her side, and with each day that passed they imbued her with fresh vigour and fresh courage. Driven back to the most distant regions of the heavens, the enemy stars could no longer reach her with their unpropitious influences, while the lucky ones found their road clear and were able to pour freely down upon her a shower of good fortune. When she thought about all this, Dora reflected that it was a kind and even touching thought on God's part, or on Fate's part, or on the part of whatever mysterious entity ruled the universe, to allow every creature a special protection on the recurring date of their birth. It was as if that God or that entity meant in some way to say to everyone: 'Don't worry, I haven't forgotten about you, nor about the fact that you are in the world by my express wish;

I so well recall the circumstances in which I sent you there that, as you see, I am still able to reproduce them with a certain amount of accuracy. It's true, I am often absentminded, I have too many things to take care of at the same time, but I never neglect to celebrate an anniversary and to entrust the heavenly bodies with some lovely gift for the fêted one.'

Such was the power to which Dora addressed herself: so good-natured, so full of paternal solicitude; and yet, this year, for the first time, his attentions were not enough to restore to her completely the faith in that happy ending which she had always deemed to be the inevitable conclusion of any misadventure. This year for the first time it seemed to her that everything she had learned to define as 'negativity' from the astrology columns not only resided out there in some far-flung corner of the firmament, but had managed to seep, if not exactly into her, at least so close as to trap her in its force-field. Oddly, the stars did not speak of any of this, perhaps because it was a negativity which was too subtle, too impalpable, to be registered by their macroscopic configurations. She herself, who for all that she lived under its insistent domination, was incapable of perceiving its nature, and she strove in vain to give it some less generic name. But there was one thing of which she was quite sure: the seat of this negativity, the centre from which it sprang, coincided with the point at which her destiny intersected with the destiny of Vulpius. At that very point the cog had jammed and given rise to the worrying grating sound, and it did not appear to have the least intention of going back to working as it should. She would have tried to talk to her friend about it had she not known in advance that he would have refused to take such reasoning seriously, dismissing it as foolish superstition. For Vulpius, she was all too aware, there was nothing that existed above man, or else it existed in a sphere that was too abstract and remote from ours to allow that assiduous exchange of flagrant and coded messages in which Dora so willingly placed her own hopes.

Thus, while Dora pondered over her own present and her future, not a word was exchanged on the matter between her and Vulpius, and each of them made ostentatious pretence of noticing nothing out of the ordinary in the other's behaviour. Regarding Vulpius, however, I should be more circumspect in charging that he pretended; it could be that he merely paid no heed to Dora's anxiety, to her bewildered looks, to the way in which, as soon as they were alone, her cheerful gabblings were stilled on her lips, to resume only with great difficulty, as if the young woman were dragging the words out of herself by physical force. Silence frightened her, whereas Vulpius seemed actually to enjoy it. He could have stayed for a whole hour in silence, sitting in front of her, observing her with those searching eyes of his or else forgetting her completely and plunging into his own thoughts.

Another detail I prefer to leave unresolved is the unknown woman's watch; it is likely that in the continuation of the story it does not reappear, which means its fate can be safely entrusted to the reader's imagination. Perhaps after that night it stayed for ever contained in the drawer, finding its definitive place among the miscellaneous deposits which had accumulated layer by layer over the years. Or perhaps from time to time, if he was alone in the room, Vulpius would bring it out and would lay it in his open palm, turning it this way and that to observe the crazy movements of the hands. Then his thoughts would go back to the unknown woman, to the night spent in the empty theatre, to the rituals celebrated daily on the stage, and he would think also of Dora, seeing her under the beam of the spotlights or in her dressing-room, as, with mechanical sureness, she carried out the laborious series of procedures which made the actress be born from the woman and then the woman again from the actress; in all of this he thought he glimpsed a figure that was still dim and blurred, yet endowed with secret coherence. It was a nameless figure, just like the negativity from which Dora sought in vain an explanation in the horoscopes, and it too was very close, almost within reach, while continuing to hide its face; but Vulpius knew exactly what he would have to do to compel it little by little to show itself, and to this end he now bent every action, every thought.

He felt exceptionally lucid, more than he had ever been in his life, and it mattered little if sometimes that same lucidity left him almost stupefied as it came to him in the form of a sinister and voluptuous intoxication. Sometimes that lucidity exhausted him, especially at night, when from behind the screen of his eyelids he could follow its enforced procedures without distraction. In the deep darkness of the room, he at times became aware of Dora's body sleeping beside him, and heard its breathing; this sound was not extraneous to the complicated symphony he was intent upon constructing; on the contrary, it fitted in with it quite harmoniously. Inspiring and expiring, systoles and diastoles belonged to the same rhythm by which his existence was now ruled, to that rigid binary rhythm which was able even to govern the most delicate mysteries of organic life. And he liked to sense its pulsations in Dora's sleeping body, he liked it to such a point that when he noticed her first signs of awakening in the morning he could not repress a start of disappointment. Then he would take refuge in sleep to pursue his own meditations undisturbed, and only much later did he resign himself to opening his eyes and embarking upon the morning's exchange of banalities with his friend.

XIV

AT LAST THE DAY of the birthday arrived. Nearly all the actors had gone down to the dining-room a little earlier than usual to leave the presents on a table cleared for this occasion, which when Dora arrived she found completely covered in multicoloured little packages. As her fellow actors, stamping their feet on the floor and tapping their forks against the edges of their plates, struck up a clamorous birthday song in her honour, she stood and gazed upon the shiny paper, the huge bows and gold string, things which for her were not merely wrappings but an essential component of the gift, and which she would open, as was her wont, with extreme care so as not to damage anything.

She wanted first to see Vulpius's gift, and she asked which of those magical containers held it; undoubtedly the prettiest, she thought, but which one was the prettiest was a question on which she could not really arrive at a definitive decision. At last she chose one with thick silvered paper and, weighing it in her hands, she shot an enquiring glance at Vulpius, who had risen from the table when the guest of honour came in, though imitated by very few of his companions. In answer to that look the young man shook his head slightly, repeating this gesture with a smile when she tried once more to guess and showed him a gaudy package on which every colour of the rainbow was amply represented.

Dora was about to make a third try, but gave up when she noticed that her fellow actors were starting to exhibit some impatience. She began opening the packages one after the other at random, and each time she appeared happily surprised by the contents, either for the sake of being nice or because those small gifts really did provoke a child's astonishment in her. They were mainly objects of no practical use, but characterised by a decorative exuberance perfectly befitting Dora's taste: the small heart-shaped enamel box, and the talking doll in Tyrolean costume, and the small jade Buddha, and the musical merry-go-round with little white horses revolving to the catchy rhythm of a famous waltz, all this she liked very much, and she endlessly thanked her fellow actors and actresses for having made her happy with such wonders. One might quibble, it's true, that the majority of these presents were more suitable for a little girl than a young woman, and Dora resented this a little, since almost no one seemed to hold a high opinion of her maturity; and yet the very few grown-up presents, a small bottle of perfume, a pair of silk stockings, a purse given by the superintendent with the wish that it might always be full, seemed to her in comparison to be dull and prosaic, and when she encountered one she had to hide her disappointment.

At last she came across a very simple package with shiny white paper. Before opening it she read the card; it was from Vulpius, written in that neat hand of his which so resembled printed characters, and it said:

> Doubt thou the stars are fire,
> Doubt that the sun doth move,
> Doubt truth to be liar,
> But never doubt I love.

Beautiful words, thought Dora, her emotion at that moment dimming her already weak memory. Splendid words; but why ever does he suppose that I should doubt his love? If he supposes it, he must have good reason. She re-read these lines and her suspicion increased. As far as she was aware, the sun did indeed stand still; her information was vaguer when it came to the stars; she would not quite be up to swearing that they were made of fire. Moreover, on a third reading she noticed that the use of the verb 'doubt' oscillated alarmingly: in the case of the sun and the stars it seemed to mean 'to put in doubt', but then, in relation to the truth, its sense was completely overturned, getting closer to 'believe' or 'suspect'. Why then had Vulpius employed such an ambiguous term, instead of making his thoughts plain and unequivocal? The more she scrutinised the card's text, the more she found it sibylline, deliberately sibylline, as if the author's only intention with this message was to disconcert her.

She was still reading when she became aware of someone just behind her. 'Aren't you going to open it?' said Vulpius, his voice very close. Dora obeyed, rather thoughtlessly tearing at that wrapping whose sobriety made it so unappealing, and in among the paper she found a little mask of black satin studded with rhinestones. She looked at it, looked at Vulpius, and as a sign of gratitude gave him a kiss on the cheek that was not altogether wholehearted; then she made to pass on to another package, but this was the last, and Vulpius was standing beside her with an air of expectancy. Dora lifted the mask. 'It's lovely,' she said, 'the card too . . . But . . .' 'But . . .?' reiterated Vulpius with a sudden note of coldness in his voice. 'Nothing, take no notice. It's really lovely.' And she put it on her face, laughing because the two oblong slits refused to coincide with the position of her eyes. At last she managed to make it fit and she turned towards her colleagues, giving a bow which they answered with lengthy applause.

At this point, the actor-manager imposed silence, and, using the tone in which he played his crusty-but-good-hearted roles, urged Dora to come to the table. If not, he asked, and this was clearly a rhetorical question, were they all to resign themselves to dying of hunger for the sake of wishing her many happy returns? If this was the guest of honour's desire, she only had to make it plain.

Dora slipped off her mask and, after turning a look of temporary leavetaking towards the presents, she made her way quickly to her place, followed by Vulpius, who gallantly pulled back a chair for her. Then, with laudable promptness, almost as if he had been poised in ambush behind the door, the waiter came in, bringing a steaming terrine of soup. 'Not for the young lady,' the actor-manager screamed as soon as the man approached Dora to serve her soup. 'The young lady would rather fast today.' You should be made aware that whenever the leading actor got hold of a joke, however feeble, he would hang on to it tenaciously like a good hunting-dog with its game bag, and this time too he kept up his embroidery on the theme of fasting and mortification even when they had reached the dessert and every one of those at table, Dora included, felt so sated that they accepted a second slice of cake as a mere matter of principle.

When the meal was over, the actors were in unanimous agreement that the time allotted to the afternoon rest should be extended by an hour. Vulpius helped Dora to carry the presents to her bedroom, and she zealously threw herself into the pleasurable task of finding the best place to arrange each one of them. At first she could not decide where to put the mask, until she had the idea of setting it on a wooden head which supported a dark-haired wig. She placed the enigmatic card in the cabinet where she kept her letters; she would have liked to ask Vulpius for some clarification, but she feared she would appear stupid or ignorant to him if she displayed her own perplexity.

However, he lingered for only a few minutes, then

excused himself, saying he was very tired, and went off, leaving her to her presents. This was what Dora was waiting for so that she could start playing her musical merry-go-round, which of all the gifts she had received seemed to her the one that promised most entertainment, and for the rest of the afternoon, until the time set for rehearsal, whoever passed by her room would hear the old waltz as played somewhat stridently by that metallic contraption.

XV

IT IS NIGHT NOW, the performance is over, and the actors are again gathered in the dining-room. At one end of the table we can see Dora and Vulpius close in conversation, their voices lowered. She laughs and shakes her head; it appears that Vulpius is telling her an improbable story or else trying to persuade her to do something out of the ordinary. From time to time their dialogue is interrupted, but is resumed almost immediately, and the more observant of their companions wonder what those two can have to say to one another that is so important, and why Vulpius especially seems really annoyed whenever someone addresses a word to him or his companion. To her, however, he speaks in a calm and patient tone, and little by little Dora's laughter and displays of reluctance become less frequent, until they stop altogether. Now, as the dessert is served, even that subdued exchange seems to be over and the two young people talk about this and that with their neighbours at table, only from time to time giving each other a look of complicity.

When the others rise, they make their way with them up the stairs and each goes to their own bedroom. As Dora passes the mirror, she stops for a moment to arrange her hair; then she takes the mask off the wooden head and slips it into her handbag. Sitting on the bed, she listens until the sound of footsteps on the stairs and in the corridors has stopped completely; then she leaves the room, closes the door and quietly turns the key.

Vulpius is already in the corridor. Allowing her to precede him, he follows her down the stairs and into the deserted entrance hall. Both of them remain silent; only once they are in the street do they begin to speak. He is unusually good-humoured, even lighthearted, but each time Dora's step slows down along the way he urges her to go on with a faint pressure to her arm. Thus quite quickly they reach the square in front of the theatre and skirt the dark building as far as the stage door. Here Vulpius brings from his pocket a key, which he shows to his girl-friend with an air of triumph, answering somewhat vaguely her questions about how he has come by it. On this point, I shall allow myself to follow his example; it is not important for us to know whether he never returned the key he had borrowed from the actor-manager that night or whether after returning it he got hold of it again, perhaps during the rehearsals, to make a copy of it. Without both-ering ourselves about this insignificant detail, we can go back to the moment when Vulpius slipped the key into the lock and once more, after so much time had passed, unlocked that nocturnal kingdom of silence which had exerted such a profound influence over him.

Dora had a moment's hesitation, then went inside, and when he had followed her, closing the shutter behind them, she found herself in the most total darkness. Her hands reached out to grope for Vulpius's arm, but she found only the void. Fortunately, before she had time to take fright too much the lights went on to reveal the long corridor with its bare walls. Vulpius was a few steps away from her, beside the switches.

'It's odd,' said Dora, 'it doesn't even seem like the same place.' 'You're right and you're not right,' he answered her. The words paired with the card's 'doubt' and 'never doubt', but Dora kept this observation to herself. She went into the women's communal dressing-room and the men's, looked at the costumes hanging up, the now melancholy mirrors in which, but for her own reflection, nothing moved, and went back into the corridor with an even greater sense of disorientation. 'I don't like it,' she told Vulpius, who either did not hear or pretended not to hear. She wanted to open the door of her dressing-room, and was amazed to discover an unwelcoming atmosphere. Lifeless and alien like this, she thought, must be how the places of their earthly existence appear to the ghosts who return to visit them across the centuries; this is why they have no peace, and why they become nasty and terrorise the living by dragging their chains or going around

with their heads under their arms. She too, should
the opportunity arise, would do something of the
kind, some flagrant action, if only to reaffirm her
presence; because, Dora realised for the first time,
as soon as we turn our back on them things tend to
forget about us, and if we take them by surprise they
greet us with detachment, as if we were intruders.

These metaphysical reflections did not prevent her
from removing two or three chocolates from a large
box she had left on the dressing-table, but they
seemed to her to taste less good than usual. She was
cheered up again when Vulpius joined her; if nothing
else there were now two of them and they could
form an alliance against the mute enmity of that
atmosphere. Yet she noticed almost at once that he
was making no substantial contribution; he ignored
all attempts at conversation, even refusing the chocolates; in short, he did nothing to dissipate the
anxiety the empty theatre provoked in her, and
indeed his proximity seemed even to make it grow,
as if Vulpius too were in some way a part of the
conspiracy of things.

Dora felt strangely alone, bereft of any help before
the unpleasant impressions that beset her, and so,
with the pretext of the lateness of the hour, she
suggested an immediate return to the boarding-
house. She suggested it with a degree of timidity,
anticipating a negative answer, and in fact Vulpius
replied that before going back she would have to
keep her promise. Then he led his resigned companion onto the stage, turned on the spotlight, raised
the curtain and disappeared, leaving her in the

middle of the set. She looked around, dispirited by the bleakness and darkness that spread out before her, so differently from the benign shadow of the hall crowded with an audience. Shortly she heard Vulpius's voice rising from the stalls: 'Now, please, you should take off your coat.' Dora protested that she was cold, but since he insisted she wound up acquiescing. A quarter of an hour, she thought, as she withdrew into the wings, half an hour at the most, then we'll go home. She removed her coat and took from her bag the black satin mask, which she put on; then she went back on stage in her low-cut evening dress. 'Here I am. What do you want me to do?' she said, addressing the dark hall. 'Say some lines.'

She racked her brains for a sufficiently long speech, and when she had found it she delivered it in the tone of forbearance used by someone humouring the whim of a spoiled child. Vulpius interrupted her almost immediately: 'Can you repeat, please?' Dora obeyed, changing her tone, but he interrupted again. 'That dress is totally unsuitable. You must go to your dressing-room and put on a costume.' 'Which costume?' she asked in astonishment. 'Any one at all.' Despite Dora's compliance, this demand exasperated her. 'I don't understand the point of all this.' 'What point should it have? It's a game.' But a game, Dora retorted in irritation, is fun if it doesn't go on for too long, and this one had gone on more than long enough. She was having no fun at all standing there alone – in the cold, what is more – merely to satisfy his absurd whims. If Vulpius wanted to see her act, let him look at her during the performances, as he did anyway a bit too often, and if this was really not enough for him, she was a sympathetic person and she would gladly have agreed to give him an encore, but in her cosy, nicely heated bedroom. What a peculiar idea, bringing her to the theatre in the depths of the night!

No answer came from the stalls. For a moment she thought he had left, but she immediately discarded that irrational suspicion; he must still be there, sitting in the front row; Dora could feel his eyes on her, as she did when he spied on her during the performance.

'I'm tired, I'm going,' she said tearing off the mask; then she heard his voice again. 'Please, wait; I'll take you back in no time at all. For now, I'd appreciate it if you would gratify my absurd whim and put on a costume. Any one you like, you can find all kinds in the wardrobe room. But, you see, that dress is an intolerable half-measure, that dress is pretending to be real . . .'

'What does that mean? After all, we're real too.' Vulpius did not reply, he merely repeated his request until Dora was persuaded that if it mattered to him so much it would be pointless and cruel not to satisfy him. Even though, to her less than brilliant mind, his reasons were destined to remain thickly swathed in mystery, she could not rule out the possibility that this incomprehensible game, like other incomprehensible aspects of Vulpius's demeanour, was a necessary stage in the development of the chrysalis. In that case, of course, she was prepared to do whatever was in her power.

'I'll be right back,' she shouted, and made her way straight to the dressing-room. After a little while she reappeared on stage wearing an Elizabethan costume; she felt a bit warmer in it than in her evening dress, and her regained well-being reinforced her altruistic notions. Vulpius, too, now seemed satisfied; sitting in his stalls seat, he went on watching her without saying a word as, her face hidden by the black mask, she spoke her lines, turning now to the auditorium, now to an invisible companion.

With an effort of imagination Dora managed to forget that she was performing before an empty hall and recovered her customary ease, although it did disquiet her that, in the absence of an interlocutor, nothing answered her words but an unnatural silence; yet it seemed to her that it was precisely situations of this kind that were received down there with particular satisfaction.

While she was engaged in one of these deficient dialogues, the lights suddenly went out in the hall, cutting her off halfway through a line. That was how she realised that Vulpius was no longer in his seat, and, turning, she saw him at one side of the stage. 'Well, then?' he said smiling. 'I hardly think it was worth the fuss of making someone plead for such a trifling thing.' She agreed with him, it was after all a trifling thing, and anyway it was over and done with; she could go home now in the pleasing knowledge that she had acted generously. Relieved, she ran to change, leaving Vulpius to wait for her in the corridor. She was in such a hurry to get out of the theatre that she even forgot to take off the mask. Only in the street did she realise, and, removing it quickly, she put it back in her bag.

A heavy downpour now fell on the town, and the two walked back to the boarding-house keeping to the inside of the pavement so as not to get wet. On certain streets the wind drove the rain directly against them, as if it was trying to push them back. When they reached the church square, it was blowing so hard that instead of cutting through they had to go round the sides, so they found themselves crossing the church forecourt. In the first, livid light of dawn the church appeared gloomy, and yet Dora thought that if the portal had been open she would have liked to go in and warm her hands at the little flames of the candles. 'It's really winter now,' she said softly, tucking her chin into her fur collar.

✥ XVI ✥

WITHIN A FEW WEEKS, the rain had turned into snow. It fell almost continuously in fat flakes to which the wind gave the shape of a dance, covering the roofs in a thick white coating which Dora could not look at without thinking of whipped cream; it piled up in ever higher mounds by the sides of the roads, which were carefully kept clear by a small army of sweepers, and it wrapped the whole town in a silence through which the voice of the church bells echoed keenly, as if resonating from a huge glass vault.

To come to the theatre the ladies enveloped themselves in fox fur and chinchilla, which were always brightened by a few white gems that then slowly dissolved during the play, dwindling to a tiny puddle of water on the cloakroom floor; the men wore fur-lined overcoats, and the repartee on leaving the theatre had become particularly laconic; even among the cognoscenti, who were usually so fierce in their defence of mutually opposing views, the frozen night air had assumed the role of a referee whose authority could not be gainsaid, and faced with which every divergence of opinion would be smoothed out with stunning rapidity.

This also fostered in them that spirit of pre-Christmas harmony which so befitted the season, making them indulgent towards actors in whom, as a rule, for the sake of argument more than anything else, they would not forgive even the smallest short-coming without picking it over in a merciless critique. Now, however, they were patently easy-going, at the most observing that for some time now little Dora had been hesitant in her movements on the stage, as if she found it a hostile environment, and she often even stumbled over her lines; but they only touched fleetingly on the subject, at once unanimously concluding that there was no serious harm after all since, though the girl had an excellent stage presence, a great actress was something she had never been, indeed her performances now were all the more entertaining, even if for unintentional reasons. What could be wrong with her? they wondered. What could be going on in her head? And without venturing an answer that would have taken them too far they quickly exchanged well-gloved handshakes and hurried off, each in his own direction, each pulling his hat right down so as to reduce as much as possible the space between it and the turned-up collar of the overcoat.

Being less chilled than they are, and less unknowing, we can take pause for longer to consider the causes of Dora's behaviour. We can understand it better if we bear in mind that after the night of the birthday Vulpius again induced his long-suffering girlfriend to accompany him to the theatre late at night, and compelled her to disport herself for him in increasingly bizarre performances. Though to start with he allowed her to speak her lines in sequence, as if she were in front of an audience, now he would become fixated on a single phrase, a single gesture, which he would ask her to repeat endlessly in an exhausting search for perfection, or else he himself would suggest very simple lines and movements to her, perhaps derived from forgotten scripts, or perhaps invented by him on the spur of the moment. Dora could not have said either way, her memory being as poor as it was, yet what was chosen seemed to her often to encompass some mocking, almost cruel intention. They were never words of love, or noble attitudes, or situations in which the character was able to express self-esteem or trust in fate, but something resembling the inchoate cry of pain, now tragic, now grotesque, from a creature surprised in its irremediable nakedness. Even if they came from a particular drama or comedy, Vulpius isolated them so as to reduce them to fundamental variations on the same theme, a theme which Dora could not have translated into precise concepts, but which in her eyes was all of a piece with the iciness of the theatre, with the unadorned stage where side-sets and backdrop renounced all seduction to exhibit their opaque material, with the darkened hall where, instead of the involved faces of the audience, all that could be glimpsed was the motionless indifference of friezes and caryatids.

That iciness, that closed-off apathy, had entered into her bones, to the point where she could not stop being conscious of them even when the theatre reassumed its welcoming face for the presence of the public and her fellow actors. Now Dora too sensed in this festively familiar aspect a simulation in which, however hard she tried, it was difficult for her to believe. Of all this, she realised, only she and Vulpius were aware, and the other actors had not the faintest suspicion that the theatre could be a place of that kind, so alien, so severe; and for all her bewilderment, the sharing of this experience with him gave her profound satisfaction, bringing him closer to her. It is true that she went on being ignorant of his thoughts, or not understanding them whenever he revealed something to her by suggestion, but she realized that they drew their primary nourishment precisely from those nights spent in the theatre, together, unknown to the other actors, like an Eve and an Adam in the solitude of a gelid paradise.

This was also perhaps why she lent herself with such surrender to the strange night game dreamed up by Vulpius; it did not escape her that now it represented the strongest bond between them, the only one that still mattered to him. A thin thread, of course, and one that could scarcely be relied upon, but if she had broken it by absenting herself Vulpius would have gone far away for ever, would have disappeared into the inaccessible hermitage of his meditations. If instead she continued to comply with him, a possible path of access would be kept open. It was not that she hoped to penetrate that hermitage – she knew she could only assume the role of a visitor allowed into the vestibule but not the inner rooms, and yet even this seemed to her better than nothing; at least, she thought, he would not be completely alone.

Yet, because her nature shrank from all that was dark and morbid in this situation, Dora felt herself intoxicated as if by a slow poison, and to endure it she had to have recourse as much as possible to the powerful antidote of normality in the daytime. She sought relief in familiar things, in the most frivolous and banal occupations; she devoted meticulous care to her appearance and went out often with her women friends on prodigal shopping trips for knick-knacks or items of clothing, which would take her mind off things for a few hours. In her bedroom she would play the merry-go-round to cover up the silence, but the notes of the waltz struck her as plaintive, touchingly defenceless, and sometimes when she heard them she was beset by an agonising sadness.

The walks she took alone in the mornings gave her greater comfort. She liked listening to the squeak of the snow beneath the heels of her little boots, and dodging the snowballs thrown by children or passing young men who could find no better way of showing her their admiration. The air was cold, to the point where it reddened her face, but this was a different cold from the one that pervaded the theatre at night. Dora distinguished between them, defining them respectively as 'live cold' and 'dead cold'; if the latter appalled her, she had always, ever since childhood, had a liking for the former.

One morning on opening the curtains she saw that the snow had stopped falling and the rooftops of the town, brightened by the sun, shone with a dazzling whiteness. Hurriedly she dressed and went out, with the idea of reaching the nearest belvedere on the hillside. With every step she seemed to shrug off the worry that had tortured her during the night; she was still, after all, the healthy and cheerful girl she had always been, and the world, too, was as it had been, a joyful mystery, a variegated amusement park which always offered new attractions to her delighted eyes. Steeples and towers with their conical plumes of snow greeted her from afar with the affectionate discretion of old acquaintances, and she returned their greeting serenely, almost happy.

The road began to slope upwards, but the slope was gentle, like everything on that sunny morning, and Dora took it easily, stopping only once to go into a café and drink a hot chocolate. Then she went on her way again, first past the houses, then through a more open landscape on which the snow was able to affirm its own dominion the more strongly, and she climbed on as far as the belvedere, an extended area enclosed by a balustrade and scattered with little benches made unusable by their thick carpeting of white.

She reached the balustrade, and shielding her eyes with a hand she set about viewing the town. From up there it was so small, so easily mastered with the gaze, that more than anything else it looked like a little model town, like the ones you see in some museums or among the toys of wealthy children; two fingers are all you need to pull down the town hall or relocate the station to where the cathedral was. Dora had not been up here for a long time, and now she had fun identifying these miniature versions of the places among which her life was conducted; she could make out the boarding-house, no bigger than a doll's house, and the church dome, which from her windows was so majestic as to inspire awe in her, now become a dainty object, a bauble to be set alongside the others on top of her chest; so tiny it was, so tiny, that she felt she was looking at one of those landscapes inside a glass ball with a snow storm ready to blow up at the slightest agitation. And the theatre, down there . . . The theatre.

Dora turned her back to the balustrade; she had stopped wanting to look. Facing her, a boy, probably a student, was smiling with his arm raised and his fist tight around a snowball. For a moment they stood motionless, opposite each other, and exchanged a look. The boy lowered his arm and hurried away, strangely ashamed, as the snowball melted in his fingers.

THE THEATRE WARDROBE WAS a low, wide room fashioned out of the area under the stage, and to reach it you had to pick your way through a labyrinth of ropes and cables. Along the walls were piled up enormous trunks in which the costumes for the different plays were put away, each one bearing a label with the title of the respective work: thus *Hamlet*, *Iphigenia*, and *The Misanthrope* lived side by side as if on the shelves of a disordered library. In the middle of the room, an ironing-board and a small table, which was always cluttered with needles, pins and reels of thread of every hue, promised to restore the crumpled contents of the trunks to their original splendour with the utmost speed, and if in the meantime, as often happened, an actor had put on weight, he could be sure that the wardrobe mistress, an accommodating soul by temperament and profession, would be able to make the old costume fit the new measurements with a few inconspicuous adjustments. For the women most of all, those visits to the wardrobe were often a source of humiliation, even if the sewing genie who reigned over it swore to maintain a father confessor's discretion about any letting out of waist or hips whose necessity proved indisputable during fittings.

When the wardrobe mistress was away, the room took on the aspect of a deserted cavern and seldom did anyone set foot there. At night it seemed altogether sinister, so that whenever Dora entered it with Vulpius in search of costumes she felt oppressed by the sight of those trunks on which an opaque film of dust had settled. They struck her as huge sarcophagi, each of which enclosed the remains of what on stage had once been life and movement, sound and colour, and now had been laid to rest inside, reduced to a pile of rags awaiting an ephemeral resurrection. What a sad place the theatre can be, she thought, watching Vulpius extracting peplums and leggings, monumental crinolines and vaporous tulle confections from the trunks. Outside, moreover, winter was particularly unrelenting, and every time it cleared the snow would again begin to fall with redoubled insistence, and she was more and more reluctant to leave her nice warm room to venture out into that uninviting blizzard. But Vulpius's will was stronger than hers, and by now Dora submitted to it with total resignation, as if in the face of a natural phenomenon or some trial imposed by destiny.

What he wanted of her could no longer be described as acting; he would compel her to stand motionless in the centre of the stage while he tried out every possible alteration in lighting on her, and each time, once the spotlights were in place, he would go down into the stalls and stay there for a long time, sitting in the front row watching that patient marionette who only every now and then would let out a yawn, or move the weight of her body from right leg to left, or in some other way display that she was congenitally unsuited to playing the part of inert matter. At moments like this Vulpius would remember Dora, the lively and naive young woman, who was fond of waltzes and chocolates, and this memory would strike him as obscuring the purity of the image which he saw on the stage. So he would hastily banish it like an intruder, an inconvenient visitor, and, after reminding his model that she was to remain perfectly motionless, return to his pursuit of contemplation; then he would climb back up on stage and take up position near the light switches. He liked turning the lights out suddenly, without giving her warning, abruptly plunging her into darkness; then the character who until that moment Dora had embodied ceased to exist, her time was up. When the house lights went on, the girl would withdraw into the wings to change her costume and the game would start all over again with a new manifestation and dissipation, a new beat in that unvarying rhythm.

So, as the night outside advanced headlong towards the luminous catastrophe of dawn, in that artificial brightness there were created and annihilated, in rapid succession, a Greek nymph and a seventeenth-century noblewoman, an ethereal little fairy in Titania's train and an ambiguous figure which beneath Don Juan's cape and plumed hat allowed a glimpse of a naked female body. With a variation in the filters, each of these labile characters passed through every shade of the rainbow, and Dora was transformed into a creature of air and water, earth and fire, and according to the systematic whim of her demiurge she became now an undersea reflection, now a fiery shooting star.

These constant alterations tired her eyes, but she endured them, partly from willingness to please and partly because she herself was intoxicated by the subtle vertigo of metamorphosis. She was happy, however, when she could finally remove the last costume and that phantasmagoria of many-hued fabrics was swallowed up again by the large, austere trunks in the wardrobe room.

As soon as she got to her room she slipped into bed and snuggled up under the eiderdown; still numbed, she slid into a disturbed and fitful sleep from which she often woke shivering. She only managed to warm up after some hours. Already, the slippered footsteps of the maid could be heard in the corridor and a bright light filtered through the drawn curtains, but Dora turned from it, towards the wall, covering her eyes with an arm; it was too early to get up; her exhausted organism demanded more rest.

She had got into the habit of missing breakfast, because she was never really awake before lunchtime; she would wash and dress in a rush and was half asleep as she went down to the dining-room, where she had had her place changed so as to be closer to the stove. Vulpius would sit at the other end of the table, and throughout the meal hardly a word passed between the two of them. But she watched him often, furtively, in that smiling, well-mannered young man scarcely able to recognise the personage who at night inspired such awe in her. In the serenity of noon, in the warmth of the great tiled stove, it seemed to her she had returned at last to reality and that the nights spent in the theatre were only a dream, a distressing one without doubt, but out of which luckily she was sure of waking each morning. Then cheerfulness regained the upper hand, and Dora laughed and joked with her companions, forgetting her cares, until she left the boarding-house on her way to rehearsals and noticed that the sun would soon be setting, and with suddenly mournful eyes she would follow its slow descent behind the rooftops of the city.

These were the shortest and most melancholy days of the year. Dora would have liked to hold back the sun, or else persuade the earth to hurry faster through its orbit to escape the dominion of that tenebrous season. Even the imminence of Christmas, which she usually greeted with a glad heart, was not enough this year to dissipate the dense fog that blanked out her joy at living; yet Dora was determined to celebrate it as usual, and one week before she had a little fir tree delivered to her room, the prettiest and most thickly clad she had been able to find.

Vulpius was with her when the tree was brought

in. He offered to help her dress it, but Dora refused; his presence would have spoiled her enjoyment. She waited, therefore, until she was alone, and after locking the door she began to explore the wardrobe and the chest in search of the box containing the Christmas decorations. At last she unearthed it, laid it on the bed and carefully took out garlands, baubles in the shape of pine cones and oranges, angels and birds with long silver tails. There had been some casualties since the year before, but the damage was limited; most of the treasure was still there, intact and resplendent, and Dora was greatly comforted by the confirmation that in the midst of all that turmoil there always still remained something which did not change, something beautiful and familiar which reappeared each year identical and invulnerable to time and the vicissitudes of human beings.

A few of the baubles went back as far as Dora's childhood, an age which she had never thought of with nostalgia, because nothing had intervened to separate the personality she had then from the one she has at this time. Yet now she felt quite suddenly different, perhaps more grown-up, if being grown-up means letting worries get you down and losing your capacity to become fully absorbed in the enjoyment of some small pleasure by firmly banishing all sad thoughts. If this was maturity, Dora saw no reason to be glad that she had reached it; and besides it did not seem to her at all that she had reached it, but rather that it had descended heavily upon her, by stealth, like a curse. That morning, when she looked at herself in the mirror, she had found on her brow the first, tiniest wrinkle. That too, she thought, was maturity, and, recalling a well-known fairytale, she compared it to an envious hag who offered young girls the gift of poisoned apples; as soon as the girl bit into the apple, farewell happiness, farewell lightheartedness, and from that moment on it was best for her not to look back at her own past, because she would no longer be able to contemplate it without regret.

From that moment on, from the moment when Vulpius unlocked the theatre door to her, Dora had no longer been the same, and now, looking at the old Christmas decorations scattered on the bed, it seemed to her again that she was looking in a mirror which gave her back an image that was altered and unrecognisable. She had even lost the desire to dress the tree, but she forced herself in the hope still of being able to find some distraction in this activity. She set to work, therefore, and very soon a resplendent spring bloomed among the dense branches of the fir tree; the garlands sent out gold and silver sparkles, the baubles splashed the tree's dark greenery with multicoloured spangles, and the small winged creatures perched motionless upon the branches, facing their captivated mistress, some with a little head that comes to a sharp-beaked point, some with a rosy countenance ringed by blond curls. Out of respect for the natural hierarchy, Dora had placed the little birds at the bottom and the angels up above, in a close-ranked succession of thrones and dominations; now, to complete her work, she had only to set the glittering comet on the top. She climbed up on a chair and bent forward cautiously, so as not to bump against the branches. She was fixing the star when she heard a knock at the door; she gave a start, and the small, precious object slipped from her hand, falling to the ground. Dora jumped down from the chair and picked it up; luckily it was not broken, but it looked cracked, and on some of the points the silver dust that covered it had been knocked off, revealing a dull, opaque surface.

The banging on the door continued more vigorously and Dora ran to open it. She found Vulpius there, come to collect her to go to rehearsals. She told him to go on down and she would meet him in the entrance hall within a few minutes; but he preferred to wait. He sat down in an armchair and glanced vaguely at the tree resplendent on the other side of the room. 'The star's missing,' he remarked. With a dejected look, Dora showed him the bruised celestial body. 'I was just about to put it on when you knocked.' 'I'm sorry I interrupted you,' he answered, 'but what's stopping you from doing it now?' 'Don't you see? It's not the same any more.'

Vulpius inspected it more carefully, running the tip of a finger over the scraped edges; then he took it out of Dora's hands and went and placed it on the top of the tree. 'From a distance,' he said as he turned to her, 'nobody will notice.'

XVIII

LET US ALLOW CHRISTMAS to arrive and go by amid festivities which we can imagine: presents exchanged, Pantagruelesque lunches and dinners at the decorated table, a persistent feeling of being over-full which makes the actors' performances rather less brilliant than usual. It is likely that on Christmas Eve the play would end somewhat earlier for the sake of all those who want to attend midnight mass. Dora is among them, and as she prays beneath the great dome she feels euphoric, because at least for today she has avoided going back to the theatre with Vulpius. Everything strikes her as extraordinarily beautiful and welcoming, even the lofty trumpeting angels cast benign eyes down upon her, and the crowd and the profusion of candles lit produce the same warmth in the church as must have reigned in the stable at Bethlehem.

The days go by, the fir tree begins to lose its needles, but it is still too early to think of taking it down. Dora is quite determined to keep it at least until the Epiphany, and every day she shifts one of the baubles or adds a garland to hide the more denuded spots, so that gradually green needles are being replaced by silver ones.

At the same time New Year's Eve is approaching, and the whole company is busy preparing for that gala night. The dark drama of love and death staged in the preceding weeks disappears from the billboard to be replaced by a comedy, for it pleases both tradition and good manners that the public should laugh on St Sylvester's night, that it should take its leave of the old year in a merry and auspicious atmosphere. One of the plays most frequently dusted down on such occasions is *The Taming of the Shrew*, and we can suppose that this time, too, preparations are underway for a staging of Katharina's grotesque sentimental education. But the public's expectations and the zealous commitment of actors and theatre staff are directed particularly to the ball planned for after the performance; the superintendent undertakes exhausting negotiations with the best wine merchants in the city to get bargain champagne, the women inspect their old evening dresses and engineer modifications which make them unrecognisable, and between one rehearsal and the next the orchestra players devote themselves with phlegmatic seriousness to going over their repertoire of waltzes and polkas.

In the circumstances, it is not surprising that there was already on the morning of St Sylvester's Day a billboard displaying the triumphant legend 'Sold Out'; for anyone who could afford it, spending New

Year's Eve at the theatre was a custom not to be forgone, and even the few subversives who craved novelty had been brought back for want of any tempting alternatives. There remained, admittedly, some unbudgeables, yet even they, had they gone past the theatre at around four o'clock and seen the pastry shop's delivery boys arrive, arms laden with packages, to disappear through the door, wafting behind them an intoxicating fragrance of *crème pâtissière* and vanilla sugar, even they, faced with such a sight, would have been overcome by the bitterest regret and would have rushed to the box office to ask if by chance anyone had cancelled their booking. But the ticket-seller, who in his heart had always disapproved of the excessive generosity shown towards the prodigal son by that biblical father, took pains to leave those eleventh-hour penitents in no doubt that he was not so lenient and that as far as he was concerned anyone who had been unable to make up their mind by now need not bother coming forward. This was indeed the unmistakeable gist of his cold 'Afraid not' muttered from the other side of the counter, and the would-be spectator had no recourse but to beat a dignified retreat, cursing his own improvidence.

The provident, on the other hand, after consuming a fairly light supper, went to take their rightful places in the theatre where at nine on the dot the curtain went up on the *Shrew*. This was a version which was drastically cut down so as not to overrun the golden measure of two hours, allowing the time to prepare the midnight toasts, and the secondary roles were reduced to their bare bones, so that Dora and Vulpius, who played the younger pair of lovers, had to make do with not many lines; for all this, it gave the young woman great satisfaction to see herself wooed by him on the stage, and it seemed to her that at that moment every woman present in the hall must envy her. It also gave her satisfaction, in the final scene, to refuse her bridegroom an obedience that was too unconditional: 'That's the way,' she said to herself as she went back to her dressing-room. 'That's how to treat men.' And she wondered why in real life she never could manage to follow this character's example.

She changed hurriedly, while the public waited in the foyer and the stage hands cleared the hall. She wore a green silk dress which was not brand new, but was freshly resplendent with long, glittering fringes of the same colour which had been stitched on in just the right places, and she finished off the outfit with two strings of cultivated pearls which had been a present from Vulpius a few years before. Then she went to the mirror and inspected herself thoroughly, even twisting her head round as far as she could so as to get a back view. All things considered, she still liked what she saw, in spite of the little wrinkle on her brow, which she had, however, cunningly covered up with greasepaint so as to make it almost invisible. Turning full circle, she tentatively sketched some dance steps; with each movement the fringes shook, rising a little as in a fluttering of wings, and it seemed to Dora that she had been changed into a bird or into one of the angels that adorned her Christmas tree. They resembled her, in fact, or she resembled them, because of her wavy blond hair and the rosy pinkness that judicious use of rouge had restored to her cheeks.

A few minutes later, a very elegantly attired Vulpius joined her and, giving her his arm, he escorted her into the hall. Only one row of seats ran under the balustrades of the boxes; the others had been cleared away, and the more impatient couples were already performing measured dance moves. On the stage long tables had been laid out with trays of cakes and sandwiches; the bottles of champagne, surrounded by sparkling glasses, awaited their moment in buckets from which the ice released thin spirals of smoke. Stiff and erect like a guard of honour alongside those dainties, the actor-manager strenuously refused all suggestions that he step down; this was his place, he proclaimed loudly, and nothing and nobody would induce him to abandon it, because an actor lives on the stage and, if need be, dies on it – instead, let the others come up and see how good it was to be there. With some colleagues following suit, he had already made a start on the propitiatory libations in the dressing-room, and now, eager to move on to the champagne, he cast irritated glances at the hands of his watch, which hobbled towards midnight with exasperating slowness.

Dora wanted to dance, and Vulpius led her to the centre of the floor. Around the young woman's waist, his arm was held totally still, with the pressure of the fingers neither increasing nor diminishing;

Dora thought that, though this controlled rigidity might well be refined, it was not over-friendly. He scarcely looked at her, but kept staring over her shoulder, and she very quickly realised that he was looking at the hall; not at the spectators or his colleagues, or the other couples engaged in the dance, but at the friezes and velvets, the cupids and caryatids, which attended on those entertainments from the distance of a disdainful solitude. He looked at them as if to re-establish a secret complicity from which all those present were excluded, or else to make sure that, despite all appearances to the contrary, the theatre was still the austere and sacred place where he loved to celebrate his rites.

Dora no longer wanted to dance. She was about to say so to Vulpius, but suddenly the orchestra fell silent and the superintendent announced that there were five minutes left before midnight. The bottles were uncorked; a lot of people went up on stage to get to the buffet and to find out, just this once, what it felt like to be up there; others, less adventurous, hung back for the waiters to come round with the trays. When midnight struck each of them took up their glass and raised it solemnly to make a toast with their neighbours.

As soon as it was settled without any shadow of a doubt that the old year was really over and the new one had been seen in and the indispensable formulas for facing that delicate transition had been uttered more than once, the superintendent gave the orchestra a nod of command to resume playing. At once there rang out the notes of a waltz which

Dora had been waiting for since the party began, her favourite, a tune that she had never been able to hear without her feet tapping. With a long-suffering air, Vulpius was busy accepting the prolix compliments of a female admirer, but would-be partners did not delay in coming forward, and their demeanour during the dance would certainly be more gallant and attentive than that of her cold lover.

Dora accepted an invitation from one of them, promising the others the next dances, and a moment later she was whirling from one end of the hall to the other in the grip of a faint, extremely pleasurable dizziness. Her partner was an excellent dancer, able to lead her and follow her so well that she readily pardoned him for not being Vulpius, and almost even ended up forgetting this. Now, inflamed by the dancing and the champagne, her cheeks burned under the rouge, and an unrestrained gaiety took her over. If the world were to end now, she thought, it would end with a flourish; and she was astonished at such a strange thought having entered her head.

The music changed, and her partner changed, without the alteration wrenching Dora out of her bliss. She was only dimly aware that the rhythm was not so fast and that her new companion had a tendency to clasp her a little too tightly round the waist, but these were quite insignificant details. She went on dancing, turning, every once in a while casting challenging eyes upon the mournful sumptuousness of the hall, upon the oppressive stuccoes, upon the statues which had seemed to her so much to be feared as she executed her nocturnal performances before them; yet she did not have to fear them, she would always triumph over them, because she was alive, her body overflowing with energy and movement, her heart knowing joy. How precious all this was, what superiority it granted her over the inert perfection of those dead things, and maybe even over Vulpius, the talented Vulpius who, however, taken up as he was with his own talent, had lost the knack of laughing and dancing and went round the hall with the stiffness of a tailor's dummy, and whenever he spoke to other people it was as if he was stretching out an arm to keep them at a distance. An unfortunate man, when all was said and done, an unhappy man; but she, Dora, was very fortunate; in a sense she was so by nature, by temperament, and she possessed such reserves of happiness that sooner or later she would succeed in conveying a part of them to her poor friend.

She saw him standing in a corner, alone, his hand tightly clasping an empty glass. At the end of the dance she shot him an enquiring look before giving her arm to her new partner; if he had wanted to dance she would have become free, but Vulpius merely signalled a curt greeting and disappeared into the crowd packed round the main exit. The orchestra struck up a polka. And yet I am happy, Dora thought. It's true, I prefer the waltz, but I like the polka too, and in life you have to know how to make the best of things. She looked at the man with whom she was dancing; he was not young but not old either, his appearance was pleasing enough. Suddenly she felt tired, so she asked him to escort her to the buffet, where she ate some little cakes and drank a second glass of champagne. The leading actor and one of the extras had gone off by themselves behind one of the flats with a bottle; they had taken off their jackets and were sitting face to face, warmly engaged in conversation. Noticing Dora, they invited her to join them, and for a moment she was tempted to accept; she then realised that she wanted to get rid of her partner.

She left with an excuse and went in search of Vulpius. She found him in the foyer, engrossed in smoking a cigarette. 'I want to go home. Will you take me back?' He put out the cigarette, offered her his arm and took her to the exit. When they were outside the theatre Dora realised that her face was streaked with tears.

XIX

THE EPIPHANY CAME AND went, and the fir tree was by now reduced to a meagre webbing of branches relegated to a corner of the terrace to wait until Dora could find the heart to throw it out; after the festive-season interval, the customary rhythm of rehearsals and performances had resumed in the theatre, proceeding undisturbed as the days outside got longer. Thus the whole of January passed and February reached almost the end of its short reign, but the chill showed no sign of abating; a layer of snow still covered the pavement, patterning faint arabesques upon it, the dirty white piles heaped up by the shovellers stood guard on the street corners, and the smoke from stoves and fireplaces that rose from the chimney-pots was the breath of the benumbed city. In the cold light everything acquired a singular exactness of outline, gradations were erased; even the passers-by who made their hurried way along the roads became totally isolated and solitary figures, bereft of any relation to what was around them. In this world of monads only the theatre continued to preserve the spirit of metamorphosis, celebrating its triumph nearly every night, when Dora went up on stage and Vulpius beamed the rays of the spotlights down on her.

I should like to make this monotonous period pass more slowly, marked as it is by endlessly unvarying gestures and movements and the repetition of the same states of mind, and to hold back the development of events in order to recreate the feeling of stasis which Dora experienced at that time, as if her life were locked inside a ring of magic, or as if the rigours of winter had also frozen the flux of circumstance by clotting it in a sheet of ice.

But our point of view is not Dora's; from our remote observation post we are able to see the water as it seethes beneath the ice, discern the small cracks that craze its surface; in the apparently halted time in which the two protagonists are imprisoned, from our post we can perceive taking shape something that is like a secret movement, a tendency, a direction. Largely hidden from the consciousness of either one, a subterranean force is gradually corroding the equilibrium which they believe is everlasting, and each day beneath their feet the ice gets thinner, the fissures deeper.

Dora now submitted to Vulpius's games with an exhausted obedience, almost as if she had lost all capacity to react, but in this weariness he seemed only to notice those aspects which favoured his plans and he rejoiced in the docility with which she had learned to give way to them. It took only heavier make-up to mask the pallor which had replaced her once healthy complexion, and if her figure had got a little sparer this change was all but unnoticeable beneath the rich draperies of her costumes.

Thus, with Dora increasingly worn out and resigned and Vulpius increasingly absorbed in these stage alchemies, they reached one night in late winter that began no differently from any other. It was still very cold, but on leaving the boarding-house Dora discerned signs of the thaw being imminent; violent gusts of wind shook the sky's fixed stillness, and the sleet that had fallen during the day was already melting. As she went along the road she felt comforted by the thought of spring's imminent arrival, for perhaps the new season would bring alteration into her life too; but as soon as she was on-stage, confronted by the unwelcoming hall, her illusions abandoned her: in there no seasons existed, time would continue its unvarying march, and she would be compelled to repeat those agonising performances ad infinitum.

Sitting in the stalls, Vulpius watched her. He had made her put on a long Greek tunic whose simplicity made it just right for catching the play of light, and when she asked him if it was not time to change her costume he answered that this one was fine and she must keep it on for the whole night. Dora did not dare to protest, even though she was shivering a little in the flimsy chiton. She stood there without moving, in anticipation of instructions, until Vulpius told her to wait for him and went off towards the dressing-rooms. He reappeared a few moments later bearing lipsticks and rouges, boxes and bottles of cosmetics which he laid out neatly on the ground, in one corner of the stage set.

Dora looked at him in perplexity. 'What's this stuff for?' 'Don't worry,' he answered, 'leave it to me.' Taking her by the hand, he led her over to this corner and set about making her up with great concentration, as if her face were the virgin canvas on which a masterpiece were to be born. He moved round her, inspecting her from all sides and making minute retouchings with the pencil or the brush, or else he would hold her chin in a kind but firm grip and shift it slightly to right or left, the better to see some detail. She did not demur, but even in passivity she felt a growing unease. 'Can I at least know what this is about?' she asked at last. 'It's a new game. See, you look sixteen now, you're a burgeoning young girl.' 'I thank you for the thought, but at my age I didn't imagine I needed any rejuvenation yet.' 'Wait,' said Vulpius, 'the game has just begun.'

He guided her towards the centre of the stage again, turned on the spotlights and stood gazing at her for a minute or two; then he came close to her with the cosmetics. Dora gave a nervous laugh. 'And now what do you want to turn me into?' 'A woman of thirty, maybe forty. It isn't hard, just a bit of emphasis on these shadows. And there's a lovely wrinkle here on your forehead . . .' She stepped back, away from him. 'I'm sorry, but I still don't understand.' 'But it's very simple: tonight I want you to let me see you run through the whole span of life, from girlhood to old age. I hope,' he went on, remarking Dora's mistrust, 'that you won't deny me this small satisfaction. It's nothing to you in the end, it's only a game.' 'A cruel game,' she objected. 'And what game isn't? Please, turn your head to the left, just a little, so that the light strikes your cheekbone . . . I can assure you that at forty you will still be very beautiful, you'll go on having flocks of admirers at your feet.'

He spoke in a low, wheedling voice, as though he wanted to soothe her, and yet Dora discerned an edge of detachment which not even the most caressing phrases could manage to hide altogether. It probably did not matter very much to him what she would be like at forty, nor how she was now; all that mattered to him was that she should stand still, and go on being as malleable as clay in the service of his slow work of moulding and shaping. Stepping back every now and then to observe the effect, he drew increasingly marked and close-lined wrinkles on her face, deepened the shadows round her eyes and spread a thick layer of rouge across her cheeks to highlight her cheekbones. Dora could not see herself, but when she met his stare upon her she was seized by an obscure dismay; this, she thought, is the look only objects have, dead and inanimate things; and it seemed to her that those cold, alert eyes were gradually stripping her of her humanity. In distress, she begged him to stop, to choose some different game. 'We've nearly finished,' he retorted. 'You must only be patient for a little longer.' But abruptly Dora jerked her chin away from his grip.

'That's enough now, I mean it: take me home.' 'I wouldn't dream of it. We haven't finished yet.'

Bursting into tears, Dora ran to the back of the stage and rushed down the stairs. Behind her she heard Vulpius's footsteps, which made her keep going; she crossed the dressing-room corridor, went outside and ran on in blind, aimless flight, as if something dreadful pressed at her heels all the way through the deserted streets of the city. She was so upset that she did not recognise where she was going, and even though she was now certain Vulpius had not followed her out of the theatre her heart was beating frantically. Looking at the world through her eyes, we would see an agitated succession of squares, streets and alleyways where now the façades of the buildings bear down on her almost to the point where they meet and bury her in stone, or now suddenly separate and leave her stranded in great wind-whipped open spaces. Seeing her, instead, from a distance, with the dumbfounded eyes of those rare passers-by who witnessed her appearance, we would see a shivering little figure dressed in a flimsy tunic, bare-armed and wearing sandals, running at break-neck speed over pavements where the melting snow had turned into greyish slush, and with a more faltering step traversing the broad circles of light formed by the streetlamps, at each crossing stopping for a moment unsure of which turning to take, and perhaps before she disappears behind the next corner we would have time to observe on her face a kind of mask, a make-up that is strikingly macabre. The passers-by imagined she was coming from a costume ball or some belated carnival party, but where could she be running in such furious haste, from what was she escaping? On this they had no means of formulating any plausible conjecture.

She herself, besides, would not have been able to give a clear answer to such questions, for there were no concepts in her mind that could have defined the sudden terror that had struck her, nor have explained it. But if her thoughts returned to what had happened in the theatre that night, to the ghastly game in which Vulpius had involved her, she felt in her bones a chill far sharper than the one that assailed her from outside, and even the deserted and tenebrous streets seemed to her reassuring by comparison with the pitilessness of the stage lights. So, seeking refuge, she plunged into them without hesitation, and felt a moment's relief at the thought that darkness would finally give her concealment; and yet she continued to sense Vulpius's eyes upon her, as if he had followed her thus far, as if there were no place nor time when it was granted to her to evade his searching scrutiny.

She wandered like this for a long time, with increasing disorientation. She slowed down only when she saw the houses become scarcer and she recognised the slope of the street that led to the belvedere; her flight had led her right to the outer edge of the city, where the last streetlamps stood guard at the frontier, and beyond it extended the black impenetrable hills, whose crests were only faintly outlined by the reflection of a sun not yet visible.

She turned back, and when she came across a cab she struggled out of her daze to hail the driver. The latter looked her up and down, stared at her face in bewilderment, then made up his mind to take her as a passenger. A funny one, that's for sure, he thought, with that horrible mask on her face, dressed more like some woodland nymph than a respectable lady; but at least, as far as he could tell, she had an address where there would at any rate be someone willing to pay the fare – she would not be able to: no handbag, and there was no way that such a garment could conceal even the tiniest purse.

Huddled up in one corner of the seat with her arms crossed over her breast in an attempt to warm herself, Dora listened to the rhythmic clopping of hooves. There was something friendly in that sound, something familiar; if she had been less upset she might have recalled certain Sundays in her child-hood, when her parents would treat the little girl and themselves to an outing in a carriage and she would find out the horse's name so that during the ride she could pay him the compliments he deserved. This time she experienced no such curiosity, and nor was she in the mood for compliments; devoid of all energy, she gave herself up to the jolting of the vehicle, finding some frail comfort in the thought that the night, thank heavens, was over, that soon she would be in her bedroom and could warm her hands at the heat of the stove, soak her feet in hot water and curl up under a mountain of blankets and eiderdowns.

The carriage jolted even more bumpily, then came

to a halt. After a few moments the door opened and the driver extended a hand to help her down. Leaning on him, Dora reached the entrance to the boarding-house and rang the bell until the porter came and opened up. She heard her own voice asking him to pay the fare; a cracked voice, which bore only a faint resemblance to her own.

'Is Miss feeling unwell?' the porter asked as he followed her into the entrance hall, he too staring at her with that air of astonishment. 'The key, please,' said the voice, and Dora went off up the stairs clutching the key in a grip that was unsure. It occurred to her that Vulpius must be back by now, that she might run into him; so she quickened her pace, while her heart began once more to beat faster, only quieting when the door of her bedroom was closed. The room was less warm than she had expected, in the stove the final embers smouldered in solitary pinpricks, and from the windows there came a light bereft of any brightness that settled on the furniture like cheerless dust.

The first thing Dora did was to go to the dressing-table; she wanted to see the result of Vulpius's handiwork. But standing in front of the mirror she did not have the courage to look. She turned abruptly, as if she herself had called out in warning of some danger; she took a few steps, stopped, and overcoming the temptation to turn back, she reached the screen, on the other side of which a basin and a jug of water awaited her. She rubbed her face with a vehemence that was almost violent, perhaps with the illusion that she could thereby erase all the events of that night. Then she collapsed on the bed, and the strength she had left was scarcely enough for her to pull the eiderdown up to her chin.

SOMEONE MUST HAVE COME in and turned on the musical merry-go-round; Dora can hear the distinct staccato sequence of the waltz notes in the silence of the room. She would like to open her eyes, but some kind of heaviness prevents her from lifting her lids. She goes on listening, and feels in no way astonished when the metallic sound of the merry-go-round is replaced by that of an orchestra. It comes from far away, yet she can make out each single note of that familiar melody, while her head is whirling in the giddiness of the dance. But she is not dancing, her body is still, stretched out on the sheet, only her fingers making a slight motion every now and then to mark three-quarter time, but for all their efforts unable to follow the rhythm of that music; their movements are too slow and uncertain, the knuckles bend with effort, and it seems to Dora that her hands have turned to lead or marble, equally inert and indifferent to the dictates of her will. And she can hardly raise the upper half of her body, her limbs are as if numbed and each time her muscles contract in the attempt to get up Dora will fall back exhausted on the pillows. A pity, because she would like to go and close the window. It is not that she is cold, on the contrary she feels as if the bed is burning and some time ago now she rolled the eiderdown off her body and lies uncovered, wrapped only in the fine linen of the tunic; but she would like to close the windows and curtains so that she need not see the bare stage through the opening, or the harsh illumined circles of the spotlights.

For a moment she wonders how she can see all this, given that her eyelids are lowered and also that the window, she is now quite certain, has never been opened. But re-establishing any logic in that world of maddened sensations is a wearying enterprise, even more wearying than trying to move, and Dora abandons it almost at once, giving in to the images and sounds that visit her in her drowsing state, receiving them just as they come, without quizzing herself.

Now the music disturbs her, penetrating her hazy consciousness like something too sharp and cutting; if only she were able to grip the pillow, to wrap it round her head and cover up her ears, Dora would stop hearing it, and she would hear no longer the beat that goes with it, a rhythmic, insistently cadenced sound, an incessant rattling in which after a time she can recognise the noise of hooves. Yes, she has been in a carriage often, as a child and more recently too, she cannot recall exactly when, but it was a black cab with huge wheels, and it rocked and jolted, and she was in a corner with her face turned to the window so as not to see Vulpius, who was sitting opposite.

Perhaps it was Vulpius who came in and turned on the merry-go-round, who opened wide the window that looked onto the stage. Dora listens to see if he is still in the room, but she can only hear the trotting of the horses, which go round and round in waltz time, faster and faster, almost smothering the music. And yet he is there, there is no doubt of it; he is watching her with those keen, enquiring eyes of his, and he has switched on the stage lights, which hurt her still, even through her closed eyelids. This is confirmed to Dora when he places a hand on her back and gives her a little shake. It seems, after all, that her body can still react, because at this contact a sudden start runs through it. The shaking is repeated as Dora wonders how it can be that Vulpius is speaking with the voice of a woman and calling her 'Miss'. But of course there is no reason, it is only a game; perhaps this is why Vulpius does not answer her, even though she is certain that she put the question in clear and audible words.

The hand is lifted away from her back; that's better, thinks Dora, at least I'll be able to sleep. She would like to slip into total slumber, free of any sensations, but she continues to hear the notes of the waltz, though fainter, more distant, while the trotting of the horses has also become almost imperceptible. At last she will be able to enjoy some peace, but a new noise unsettles her, a clamour coming from the corridor. She can make out the leading actress's affected drawl, the shrill tones of her other women colleagues. What do they want from me? There's still time before rehearsal starts. Now they are close, bending over her, drawing ice-cold hands across her brow. Someone covers her up, and Dora struggles in vain to protest; they seem not to hear her or else not to understand, and the more she moves about, the more they tuck the eiderdown all round, imprisoning her in its raging hot embrace.

If nothing else, they have managed to silence the music and the hoofbeats altogether; the only thing to be heard in the room is the strangely muffled sound of their voices. They murmur reassuring words, and Dora cannot understand why they do this; what she needs are not reassurances, but sleep, for a long time, maybe till tomorrow. Yet, if they want to stay, let them, let them go on talking in that sing-song tone that lulls her so gently. Who knows what they are saying? Dora no longer takes any interest, these discussions are too complicated for her to be able to follow them, and fortunately no one appears to expect an answer from her; so gradually she takes refuge in sleep, or rather in a daze where the voices scarcely reach her, as if they belonged not to the present but to some remote and muddled region of memory. By degrees she feels herself sink into unconsciousness, and her body too sinks, submerged by torpid billows from which she resurfaces at ever greater intervals, until this involuntary resistance is crushed once and for all and she can yield, with nothing standing in her way, give in to the fluid spell of dissolution.

Abruptly she is roused; someone's fingers have gripped her pulse and keep hold of it for a long time, then this person lifts her up from the waist and knuckles strike on her chest and her back. They do not seem like women's hands, they are bigger and their touch is less delicate, and the voice speaking is the voice of a man. Perhaps Vulpius still wants to go on playing, does not realise how exhausted she is. She tries to escape his grip and let herself fall back on the bed, but he holds her back firmly. Now he is pressing something freezing cold against her chest, perhaps an ice cube; he takes it away, then presses it back following the outline of her breast and then along her shoulder-blades, and Dora wonders why it is that her women friends don't make him stop but pander to him in every way and speak in such tones of respect. She can understand scarcely anything of what is said, catching from the man's lips only a few words such as 'serious', 'cold', 'delirium', without being able to establish any intelligible connection between them, yet she realises that this is not Vulpius's voice. So, she thinks, this is not some new game; and with trustful surrender she lets herself be supported by that unknown arm. Then the man takes the little cube of ice away from her body and slowly settles her back on the pillows.

✣ XXI ✣

THAT NIGHT, AFTER DORA had run off, Vulpius lingered for some time in the theatre. He turned off the spotlights and put the cosmetics back in the dressing-room, making sure to tidy everything away, but his actions were mechanical, unthinking, like those of someone brusquely roused from a thrilling dream. Only when he was out in the fresh air did he regain some self-awareness and the enchantment in which he was caught slacken its grip, allowing him to turn his thoughts to Dora and her surprising reaction. He was overwhelmed by a profound anxiety at the possibility that the young woman might definitively shun the celebration of those rituals, yet he still felt sure he could put things right and elicit obedience from his recalcitrant partner.

He gave no thought at all to her state of mind or what might have happened to her in the course of that sudden flight. He was selfish, I do not wish to deny it, with a selfishness which will perhaps appear monstrous, but which becomes almost inevitably second nature in one who is to such a degree under the sway of an obsession that he regards as irrelevant, by comparison, his own person and that of others, his own well-being and that of all those close to him. In demanding those sacrifices of Dora, Vulpius had as his goal not pleasure or happiness; those were things he had long since renounced, perhaps right from the evening when the curtain had risen on *Don Juan* and his gaze had met the dark and shining eyes of the unknown woman, or from when the demon that ruled over his destiny had brought him for the first time into the nocturnal solitude of the theatre.

Ever since then, what Vulpius had sought, what he had pursued with the systematic tenacity of madmen or heroes, had no longer borne any resemblance to the infinity of desirable aims towards which men can direct their efforts. It was a solitary and paradoxical path guided by instincts altogether opposed to that of self-preservation, and gradually as he advanced along it he became deaf to life's appeals and shouts of warning. Dora's performances constituted an essential stage on this path; by establishing the ephemeral, elementary plot for the characters she embodied, it seemed to him that he was entering deeper and deeper into the secret rhythm of things, grasping its charm and its cruelty, making himself its accomplice rather than its victim. So, just like a priest conducting the liturgy, he complied with and repeated the ever-identical gesture of that divinity of whom his intuition would show him a glimpse behind every motley appearance both inside and outside the theatre. All the images created upon the stage by his tyrannical imagination, all the incarnations to which Dora lent her own body, achieved a certain truth only at that moment when he switched off the spotlights and chased them back into the darkness, and each time he would prepare for this moment with care, and would celebrate it like an apotheosis.

Since in his eyes this game bore the imprint of necessity, the notion that Dora should put an end to it seemed to him as unlikely as that she should be able to stop the movement of the planets by raising a hand. He therefore returned to the boarding-house with his mind at rest, and it did not even worry him when he saw that the light was out as he passed her room; Dora must have already gone to bed, and it would be better if he did not disturb her; in the morning, clear-headed, she would realise that she had behaved absurdly and would let herself easily be persuaded to go back to the theatre.

Comforted by this certainty, Vulpius went to bed and almost at once sank into his customary heavy sleep, from which he was awakened only in the late morning by the sound of footsteps and voices, an unusual commotion that came from the corridor. He hurriedly put on a dressing-gown and looked out of the door: the women of the company were gathered together, swarming feverishly round a masculine figure in whom he immediately recognised their trusted doctor. He took a step towards them, but as soon as the leading actress caught sight of him she threw herself upon him and took his hands, fixing him with one of her most tried and tested tragic expressions. Then, slowly, I dare not say whether to soften the blow or to exploit to the full the effect of a gradual revelation, she told him that in the morning, her suspicions aroused by the strange silence which emanated from the room and by the porter's strange story, the maid had repeatedly knocked on Dora's door and finally, receiving no answer, had made up her mind to go in. Seeing the girl lying on the bed in the grip of a wordless delirium, she had called for help, and she herself, the leading actress, had come running with her colleagues. She had only needed one look to grasp how serious the situation was; thanks to her celebrated presence of mind, without a moment's delay she had sent someone to fetch the doctor. Why was it that she had not thought of alerting Vulpius too? Well, there was no reason to alarm him yet, it might after all be just a passing malaise; and then, she added in an undertone, she was afraid of committing some indiscretion, because according to the porter's account Dora had spent the night out, coming in only at daybreak, and the most puzzling thing was that when they had found her she was wearing a stage costume, exactly that, a peplum or a tunic, in short, one of those devilishly shapeless Greek tragedy things that leave you not knowing where to put your head or your arms.

As soon as he was able, Vulpius interrupted this detailed report and went up to the doctor to ask him if Dora's condition gave cause for concern. The man answered that it was certainly not good, talked of a high temperature and pulmonary inflammation, and ended by exhorting Vulpius to be brave and await further developments with resignation. It was still too soon to say, there could still be a turn for the better, although he personally was disinclined to build up the friends' hopes too much. In any case, he would be back to look at the patient that afternoon.

With his women colleagues by his side, Vulpius entered the room. Dora lay with her eyes shut, her chest covered with a steaming poultice. They had taken off her Greek tunic, deeming it an outfit which was unseemly for one seriously ill, and had slipped on a severe piqué nightdress which he did not recall ever having seen before. On her oblivious face he glimpsed something that simultaneously dismayed and fascinated him, an aura of sacredness, as if this very ordinary girl, whose eyes had never looked out beyond small, everyday concerns, had all of a sudden been admitted into a more elevated realm which was still barred to him.

He sat down at her bedside and continued to look at her with admiration, even with a tinge of envy, taking no notice of the women's comings and goings as they tried to shake her from her torpor with the most peculiar procedures. At lunchtime they urged him to go down to the restaurant and eat at least a little something, since misfortunes, it is well known, are better endured on a full stomach, and besides the poor girl did not need to be attended by so many people, they could easily take turns. But Vulpius firmly refused to leave her side and remained there all afternoon, taking only a few biscuits from the comfort cupboard and greeting as unwelcome intrusions the visits of the doctor and all those who came to enquire about Dora's health. This attitude was viewed by his colleagues as the sign of a legitimate despair, and they considered it natural that he should defect from rehearsals; only in the evening did he appear punctually at the theatre to perform his part in the play, while Dora, still unconscious, was entrusted to the care of the boarding-house landlady. When the curtain went down he changed at furious speed in order to run back to her, and I would like to believe that it was affectionate solicitude which impelled him, or perhaps remorse at having been the cause of this calamity. It is likely that these sentiments truly did influence his conduct, and Dora's return to health, we know, was close to his heart for more than one reason, but in his searching gaze on her there could be read neither the tenderness of the lover nor the guilty man's contrition.

Once back from the theatre, the other actors joined him and lingered for some time, soothing the patient with consoling phrases and promises of speedy recovery which she was unable to hear; then they tiptoed away to go to the restaurant, and during the meal they unburdened themselves and dissected their shared affliction under all its aspects, regretting that not even now was there a way of inducing Vulpius to join their grieving table. Alone, in the room lit only faintly by the light of a single bedside lamp, he did not shift his gaze from the hieratic white mask that seemed to cover that face. It was deep night by now, the hour when they were usually together at the theatre, and Dora was staging a brand-new performance for him.

All of a sudden, greatly perturbed, he realised that the mask had opened its eyes and was watching him in its turn. There was no mistake about it, it looked at him dimly but consciously, and its lips moved as if attempting to speak. Vulpius drew closer, bending over her; now a faint murmur was audible, and putting his ear to her mouth he managed to make out Dora's words: 'How long?' she said. 'How long will you keep on staring at me?'

Vulpius did not reply. He placed a hand on her burning brow and stayed there, motionless, kneeling beside her, until her eyelids fell shut and Dora vanished back into the closed universe of her delirium.

❖ XXII ❖

I SHOULD LIKE TO be able to spare Dora's life, to describe her slow recovery and then perhaps have her leave, sorrowful, yes, but free at last. She would flee far away from Vulpius, moving to another city, one equipped with a municipal theatre, where gradually she would reconstruct the lacerated fabric of her customary life, and her carefree temperament would once again prevail and cancel out the memory of that winter.

Unfortunately this solution is impracticable, and not just because with the passing of the hours the doctor's opinions allow diminishing room for hope; however regretful and however resistant the author might be, the plot's own development by now imposes the sacrifice of Dora, and from necessity, therefore, we must adjust to doing without this character, to forsaking her childish passions and her superstitions, her naivety and her sufferings. All this and everything else which we can encompass under Dora's name was swept away one morning, three days after the illness began, or rather snuffed out, because the wind that threatened to ravage her spent life met with no more resistance than that of a feather. Thus, without even being aware of it, Dora let herself slip into death, while her fellow actresses sobbed, the actors furtively dried their tears and Vulpius's thoughts teemed feverishly on the threshold of that alien world in which she had found refuge, as he tried in vain to catch sight of whatever lay on the other side.

The curtains were drawn, but through the gaps what was by now a spring sun attacked the room's penumbra with blades of vivid light. Sitting all round the bed, those present spoke in low tones so as not to disturb Dora, whom the most sentimental among them had observed seemed not dead but merely asleep, in a deep slumber in which she had without doubt attained the peace denied to those still breathing. Half an hour later the doctor arrived, and after a quick examination he certified the conclusive nature of that slumber; then he went off, accompanied by the actor-manager, who had assumed responsibility for making the funeral arrangements, and the others stayed on to watch over the corpse.

This vigil lasted two days and two nights, and little by little, by some tacit agreement, the actors' conversation moved away from the recent calamity to return to the subjects of old. These serene creatures of habit lacked the capacity to endure for too long any meditation upon the frailty of earthly things dictated by circumstance, and they were convinced, moreover, that not even Dora would have found this to her taste. If she had been able to speak she would have urged them to be cheerful, to make no surrender to affliction, and they tried with all their might to follow these precepts, although each time they looked at the corpse the words would fade on their lips and the foreboding of annihilation run through them like a shudder, reducing even the most loquacious to silence. For this reason, as if they hoped thereby to mount greater resistance to these sudden assaults, they sat closely gathered together in one corner of the room, and each of them sought comfort in the presence of the others.

Only Vulpius was apart from them, at Dora's bedside, following the slow metamorphosis of her face, which became increasingly rigid with the passing of time; he even had difficulty believing that it could have been animated by any expression at all, so much did its fixity strike him as an everlasting and inescapable state. Her lips were slightly parted in a frozen ecstasy, as if in her last moments it was granted to Dora to glimpse what approached to destroy her. Perhaps for this reason, because under her lowered lids she guarded the memory of such a vision, to him she showed herself to be more beautiful than she had ever been; her somewhat touching flirtatiousness and the disordered high spirits of her gestures had been soothed into an image which already seemed sculpted in the marble of a funeral monument, and Vulpius felt confirmed in his belief that stillness was superior to movement, death to life. Thus the macabre spectacle from which the others averted their eyes in horror was for him a miraculous transfiguration; before disappearing into nothingness, Dora was ascending to that ineffable purity which is not of human beings but only of crystals and statues, of that which has never possessed any life or has separated from it.

Before her inert body he experienced a kind of veneration, which increased on the day of the funeral, when Dora was laid out in the coffin. Dressing her, the women friends had found nothing more suitable than a long black gown studded with sequins, which shivered with a live sparkle in the light of the candles lit by the sides of the bier. All around, wreaths and bunches of flowers waited to follow her into dissolution or to set their stubborn hues against it. Vulpius feasted his eyes on the pomp of these funeral preparations, and failed to understand why his colleagues were intimidated by it; in the ceremonials of death there were many aspects which closely recalled the theatre, or perhaps the converse was true; in any case, a kinship existed between the two, a subterranean affinity, and in the darkened entrance hall of the boarding-house Dora was parading the last of her costumes.

She seemed to be playing the part of a queen: haughty and dignified, she received the homage of the survivors who filed awkwardly past the catafalque, glimpsing something unseemly in their being alive. Then the sparkle of the sequins, the white arms folded on her breast, the hair spread out on her pillow in the shape of some expert embroidery, all disappeared beneath the lid of the coffin, which was hoisted onto the funeral carriage amid general pathos. Vulpius refused to go to the head of the cortège, even though the others took the view that, given his relationship with the deceased, this position fell to him by right; he preferred to hide away among the small crowd, made up in equal parts of actors and audience members, which filed behind the rocking carriage through the city streets. Only when they were in the church-square did he approach and shoulder the coffin along with three of his colleagues. He had not imagined it to be so light; it was as if it contained only an evanescent residue of Dora's body.

The coffin was set down before the high altar and Vulpius withdrew to one of the back rows. Around him the great oval space of the church decked out in mourning was enfolded in the same penumbra that precedes the start of performances in the theatre, but the glow from the candles lit on the altar made the gilded stuccoes shine and spread a patina of light across the heavy black draperies. Here at last it seemed to him that his woman friend's death had found a worthy scenario, a faultless and seamless production fit to exalt its mystery. Even his fellow actors had abandoned their clumsy pose of dilettantes struggling with an especially demanding script, and were now responding perfectly to the liturgy being conducted by the priest.

Vulpius did not take part in the prayers, did not join the choir of the faithful; he attended this performance as a mere member of the audience, yet he drew from it a meaning which the others could not grasp, even though they helped in its creation. A different voice spoke through their voices as medium, addressing itself solely to him, turning those litanies into a coded language. Perhaps only the woman shut away in the coffin was able to interpret it fully, and with her the unmoving creatures who inhabited the church, the angels and winged cupids, and the courteous gentleman armed with his scythe; but it must have been known above all by another character whose detached presence he noted now for the first time, a St Sebastian who looked down with entranced eyes on the arrows that transfixed him. Like Dora's, his lips were parted, and in their marble lineaments there shone a secret rapture. It was this same mournful excitement which pervaded the whole church, which animated the heavy spirals of the columns in their restrained impulsion, which vibrated in the sacred forms of words delivered by the priest. Frailty had wished to cloak itself in the most solemn vestments, in the richest of costumes, when it showed itself before the might that was destined to destroy it, and it bent towards this destruction with an unconquerable yearning, was drawn to it and fascinated by it, went to meet it with the blind attraction that guides the moth towards the flame.

Under the compelling influence of that rapture, the faithful gathered round Dora's coffin sang at the top of their voices, forgetful of her and of themselves. Yet, what measure there was in that singing, what circumspect artifice; the ritual unfolded with ineluctable precision, with gestures and cadences, thoughts and feelings, stripped of every personal aspect in order to rise to an abstract dimension where nothing but disembodied meaning was left. In that ritual and in the temple which mirrored it there was no nature, only a sumptuous, fleeting web of appearances without substance, the manifold repetitions of an abdication of being before nothingness. Perhaps for this reason, despite their immobility, the statues that Vulpius could see seemed to him oddly unstable, bereft of duration; if the material that imprisoned them should for a moment slacken its grip, they would fail to maintain their precarious equilibrium, they would disappear almost instantly, in the same way that characters on stage disappear when the curtain comes down. The eternal life that the priest was pronouncing at the altar was contradicted even by those marble faces, by those bodies immune from pain; even for them, only death could be eternal, a total death without promises before which the world bowed with all the magnificence of its ceremonial.

Dora had attained an eternity of this kind, one more inscrutable than any paradise; and so the liturgical splendour could spread out around her body as around a relic, and the haughty throng of statues could welcome the little parvenue with indulgence. Now not even her fellow actresses dared to weep for her; fully conscious of its atmosphere, they followed the ritual in the most scrupulous manner, and the men, too, who before going into the church had expressed their bereavement in energetic noseblowing, now maintained a stance of austere dignity.

Vulpius looked at them one by one, surprised and amused by this transformation. Nearly all of them had taken their places in the pews, with only the few unbelievers and those who professed a different faith remaining unseated near the portal, in visible conflict between intellectual detachment and the intimate involvement of feeling.

All of a sudden, Vulpius had the impression of being similarly watched. His scrutiny went from one group to the next, but he met no one's gaze; the general focus of attention was what was happening in front of the altar, neither the faithful nor the atheists paying the slightest heed to his person. And yet he continued to feel he was being watched, and his memory brought him a sharp recall of those nights in the theatre, when the eyes of the unknown woman had carved out for him an intangible domain of solitude and silence amid the animation that ruled on the stage.

Slowly, with timorous caution, he looked around, his eyes exploring every corner, striving to discern things even where the darkness was most dense, and finally he glimpsed an isolated figure which stood out only faintly from the half-shadow by the holy water font; he saw the low-necked black dress, the hair loose on the shoulders, the shining eyes that held his gaze with untroubled sureness. So she had returned, though not to the theatre, but to an occasion both so different and so like, taking him by surprise and yet allowing him to suspect a necessity, a correspondence with his state of mind and his desires.

If until then Vulpius had assisted at the liturgical performance staged around the bier only as a spectator, now suddenly he felt himself to be a part of this performance which was being enacted for that single watching woman, invisible to the other actors. Like the sequin-studded gown which covered the corpse, the unknown woman's attire was more suitable for a first night than for a funeral ceremony; and yet the bare arms, the unadorned white breast, the lucent fabric shot through with reflections, made an image whose every detail seemed permeated with the mournful splendour of the church, absorbing it and irradiating it back to itself with redoubled intensity.

Almost without his realising it, as he gazed at her Vulpius's lips began to form the words of the prayer. He did not understand them, he did not interrupt his own thoughts for them, all he did was recite them, and she listened closely to the lines of that script. Gradually, as the service drew to an end, Vulpius experienced a growing anxiety. He would have liked to reach the unknown woman, to prevent her from escaping him again. What held him back was not merely his fear of disturbing the ceremony and calling attention to himself from those present; even if there had been no obstacle of that kind he would have found it hard to move, because that gaze cast him into a hypnotic rigidity, weighed down upon him with the weight of a spell.

He therefore remained in his place, torn between inertia and apprehension, nor did he get up even when the mass came to its end. She went on staring at him, without either moving away or coming towards him; Vulpius tried to rouse himself, but he did not dare traverse the distance created between them by the cold glimmer of her eyes. Meanwhile the congregation was crowding towards the portal, and it very soon surrounded the unknown woman, blocking her entirely from his sight. When the double doors were opened the sudden light dazzled him so that he had to screen it out with one hand, and it took him a few moments to distinguish anything in that brilliance. At last he could see the small crowd thinning out, the men and women dressed in black disappearing one after the other into the rectangle of bright light; but as soon as the way was clear, Vulpius realised that the unknown woman had disappeared with them.

Dazed, he went on sitting in the pew until someone shook him lightly by the shoulder; he turned and saw the actor-manager standing behind him. 'Are you planning to let us know what's the matter?' he asked, looking him up and down with an air of reproach. 'We're waiting just for you so that we can move the coffin.'

XXIII

IN THE WEEK FOLLOWING Dora's burial the members of the company set about erasing the traces of her earthly sojourn; the bedroom had to be cleared to make room for new occupants, and everything she had accumulated over the years was either thrown away or shared out among those who were left. The little domestic altar with its photographs of her father and mother was dismantled, the comfort cupboard was emptied, and the actresses dried their tears as they reviewed her clothes in the hope of being able to adjust them to their own figures. For himself Vulpius took only the small black satin mask; he took it to his bedroom and laid it in the drawer where he kept the unknown woman's watch, then he returned to help the others with that melancholy removal, until there was nothing left in the room that recalled Dora's existence. After the others had left he lingered for a few moments longer, contemplated the denuded walls, the empty, wide-open wardrobe, the plainness of the furnishings now that they were no longer hidden by the profusion of bric-a-brac with which she had liked to surround herself, then he went out, closed the door and took the key downstairs to hand it in.

Thus Dora departed once and for all from the circle of the living, leaving nothing more of herself than an affectionate memory and a few keepsakes scattered here and there among unfamiliar objects, and we find ourselves alone with Vulpius, with this dark and disagreeable character, and now suddenly bereft of the screen that allowed us to cast an indirect glance upon his obsession. The time has come for us to look straight at it, because Vulpius is now centre-stage, ready to take on the role of overriding protagonist. It is true that there remain the actor-manager, the superintendent, Doña Elvira, and others whom I could draw out from the indistinct chorus of the company, but these are nonetheless secondary figures destined to be driven ever further into the margins by the subsequent development of the plot. So it seems inevitable that at this point the author's visual angle should coincide with that of Vulpius, and I am almost tempted to identify with him, to superimpose his voice over mine, so that from now on it would be the hero himself who would say 'I' and his thoughts and the movements of his soul would be transferred onto the page without any mediation.

All the same, I am prohibited from exercising such a choice by a deeprooted mistrust of immediacy, which Vulpius would undoubtedly share. The point is that I must narrate a delirium, not be delirious, and, though the other screens have fallen, the use of the third person still always permits the preservation of a healthy detachment, the giving of shape and order to the inner magma of the protagonist. Perseus did not look at Medusa's petrifying face in its reality, but regarded its image in a mirror, and in this way succeeded in approaching it without losing himself; by adopting a not dissimilar precaution, we shall follow Vulpius's story to its conclusion through the reflection of a narrative voice, penetrating the most secret crannies of his heart and yet remaining separate, in that position of estrangement and omniscience from which, outside the conventions of the novel, only God or the gods may observe the vicissitudes of humanity.

Besides, in the preceding pages we have sometimes made use of this divine gaze, managing to glimpse something of the intense fervour that Vulpius concealed behind the coldness of his demeanour. Certainly, it was a fervour of the mind rather than of the feelings, an intoxication of concepts and reckless links of logic, and perhaps it did not really contradict that coldness, but emanated from it; after all, even ice burns, and the dogged rigour of reasoning sometimes leads to exaltation and madness. So, in the days that followed the funeral, Vulpius felt like a mathematician who was now close to discovering a theorem of major significance, and he worked out and re-worked the givens in search of the definitive formula. The church and the theatre, the liturgy of death and that of make-believe, between all these there must exist some precise connection, some exact correspondence, and thus one even between the pale figure of the unknown woman and the equally pale figure he had seen in the coffin, with her black gown and her arms folded on her breast, no longer little Dora but a different character, an exceptionally important one, in relation to whom any form of familiarity had become at a stroke inconceivable.

This connection was what he strove to grasp as he performed with the others, increasingly indifferent to the fact that besides the caryatids and cupids there was a flesh-and-blood audience attending the plays, and all the more so at night, when he went back alone to the theatre and looked around with a yearning recollection of his model's docility. Now it was he who had to go up on stage, put on the costumes, expose himself to the beams of the spotlights; he had already realised this at the funeral when he felt suddenly upon him the penetrating gaze of the unknown woman. For Vulpius too Dora's death meant that a screen had fallen away. Thanks to his girlfriend, through her, for a time he had managed to employ deceit and self-deception, to make his own votive offerings without offering himself; in this and only in this did he now recognise a fault, that of having sent Dora ahead, an unknowing explorer, on the path assigned to him. This he tried to remedy, night after night remaining on stage for as long as his endurance allowed, often turning towards the proscenium box to try to discern in the thick darkness which filled it that which was not there and could not be there, the absent watching woman to whom he dedicated those phantasmagorias.

Although, despite her disappearance at the end of the ceremony, he had cherished the faint hope of seeing her again at performances, it took him only a few days to become disabused. It may be that from the start he went back to the church from time to time while mass was being celebrated and examined one by one the women there absorbed in prayer, or it may be that he never went back again, sensing that the unknown woman's appearances were not dictated by chance, still less by the will of her favourite, but followed some strict plan. As soon as this demanded it she would show herself again; in the meantime it was pointless to seek her out, and very soon Vulpius resigned himself to waiting with total passivity, without trying in any way to force the course of events.

Nevertheless, the vision of the church came continually into his mind, especially when he happened to be in the theatre, and its gilded splendour would merge increasingly with that of the stuccoes which ornamented the hall, the funeral panoply with the heavy velvet of the curtain and the drapes, the candle-lit altar with the stage where every night, beneath the spotlights' beams, the world would hide its own vanity while proclaiming it in a ritual that was no less resplendent and solemn. In Vulpius's frenzied mind the two images converged to the point of being identical, erasing the boundary between memory and perception; they joined in the perfect solidity of a single sphere, and I could not say which of them was at its centre, whether the unknown woman's empty box or the coffin before which the priest recited the sacred lines of his script.

✣ XXIV ✣

THE SPRING SO IMPATIENTLY awaited by Dora had
arrived, the parks and gardens had some time since
undergone their resurrection, and with the breeze
there came down from the hills a soft scent of grass
and flowers. That timely reawakening of life modi-
fied the habits of the municipal actors to only the
smallest degree; in the restaurant the big majolica
stove was unlit and the greater variety of fruit and
vegetables gave irrefutable proof of the new season's
superiority over its predecessor, but otherwise
nothing had changed; their existence continued
unfolding almost always in seclusion, and the idea
of venturing out on a walk other than the usual
route between the theatre and the boarding-house
did not even cross their minds. If the sky threatened
rain a basic prudence counselled staying where there
was shelter, and if it was a fine day, why spoil it by
subjecting oneself to exertions and discomforts
when you could enjoy it well enough by looking
out of the window or stepping onto the balcony

from time to time? At the most, after rehearsals they would go and sit at the little outdoor tables of a café where they would have an aperitif accompanied by generous helpings of olives and cocktail snacks; they sprawled in the chairs, took deep breaths, and considered with satisfaction the benefits that this open-air life would bring to their health. So long as one did not overdo it, of course: excessive amounts of oxygen could in fact turn out to be harmful, but fortunately the atmosphere of the dressing-rooms, saturated with dust and cigarette smoke, would very quickly ensure that the right balance was restored.

Vulpius had never belonged to this school; he liked walking, and even the year before he had greeted the advent of spring with long strolls in the town parks, either alone or with Dora. Now, however, he seemed to share the other actors' incurable claustrophilia, and, whereas the latter were concerned only to maintain contacts with the external world within the limits of judicious moderation, he tried to avoid such contacts as much as possible. He could not bear to be outside, and the sight of nature, or of the timid fragments of it that are offered to the eyes of those who live in cities, had the effect of being even hateful to him. There was something false, something desperately false, in the exultation with which organic life celebrated its ephemeral victory, almost as if it had forgotten the nothingness from which it came and to which it was destined to return. How much greater was the dignity showed by the dead flowering of the stuccoes, the serene indifference of the caryatids! By now Vulpius was spending almost the whole day in the theatre, tolerating the intrusions of actors and spectators with an ill-concealed annoyance. As soon as the curtain went down he would shut himself in his dressing-room and wait for the others to leave so that he could regain possession of his own domain, where he would linger on until dawn, no longer taking care to keep this habit secret. For a while now, moreover, his colleagues had stopped knocking on the door and urging him to go back to the boarding-house with them; his absence from the table at the restaurant had become such an accustomed event that it provoked no surprise, and all of them showed themselves willing to forgive him this outlandish behaviour: since poor Dora had said farewell to the world, Vulpius had no longer been the same, one had to be patient until he came round and for now let him do whatever he felt like, however much his actions seemed to contradict good sense.

Thus they refrained from asking him any questions if they arrived in the theatre and found a spotlight still lit or a prop forgotten at the front of the stage, and the wardrobe mistress too did no more than make mild remonstrances over the havoc he wreaked in her realm. Once, however, as they were on the point of rehearsing some jolly comedy, they found the leering skull of Yorick in the centre of the stage, and after exhausting all suitable good-luck conjurations the actor-manager decided to submit the young actor to a vigorous scolding: enough was enough, until now they had tolerated all his eccentricities in silence, but tolerance, too, was something not to be abused, and Vulpius had gone too far. He was so enraged that he addressed him with unaccustomed politeness, using the formal modes of address that he only adopted with colleagues in quarrels. Perhaps, he said, to general approbation, the gentleman had forgotten that he was not the only one there to possess a sensibility and a nervous system, for which reason he himself was taking the liberty of refreshing his memory. If it was not too much trouble, he begged him to refrain in future from exposing the others to sights that were macabre and unlucky; it was quite enough and more to have to fiddle about with that skull once a year when they did *Hamlet*; otherwise, it was best kept locked in its trunk and Vulpius had best do the decent thing and leave it there.

The young man answered this tirade with vague words of apology and lost no time in carrying off the cause of the scandal. No one ever referred to the episode again, the actors resumed their customary show of indulgence, yet from then on their compassion was mingled with a tinge of fear, as if at a stroke Vulpius had changed into a stranger. And indeed he had chosen his companions elsewhere, day after day behind the backs of the living, strengthening his alliance with very different beings, composed of heavy, inert matter or of the evanescent kind from which there rise the figures of imagination. Nor in the unclear light of recollection did the unknown woman seem to him of flesh and blood, but something halfway between a statue and a ghost, concrete and peremptory and yet always on the point of vanishing, and he ascribed Dora to the same stock, at least as adoptive daughter, ever since he had seen her on her deathbed elevated to that marble-like solemnity. He could now trust only creatures of this kind, removed from the perpetual idle chatter of earthly existence; each night for them he staged his performances, whose exclusive subject was precisely the nature of such women onlookers and the tormenting nostalgia which increasingly drove him towards them.

I have used the plural in obedience to our logic whereby Dora and the unknown woman, the caryatids supporting the boxes and the statues lurking in the deep gloom of the church make up a multiplicity of different elements, but for Vulpius it was not like this; *his* logic saw in them more or less clear and complete manifestations of the same entity, and if we wished to respect it we would need to speak of a single female onlooker, omnipresent and yet hidden, evoked by him on stage in every gesture and in every line.

Although she was wary and aloof, and granted a partial view of herself only in isolation and silence, Vulpius was conscious of her gaze even when the hall was packed, and the other actors took pains on stage to offer their unwitting homage to her. Then, seeing that everything inclined towards her even without knowing her, he realised how great was her power. He would not succeed in escaping it even had he wished, for where can you escape that which is locked into every thing and every soul like the farthest-reaching, most intimate and secret word?

But Vulpius did not wish to escape her, he wished to serve her with devotion, and as he moved among his colleagues he felt a desperate pride at the thought of being the first and the most faithful of her acolytes.

If the others had guessed anything of these thoughts, Vulpius's new strangeness would have certainly assumed a much more ominous appearance in their eyes; but even as it was, the fact of performing alongside him amounted to a danger, so remote did he seem: he scrupulously adhered to the requirements of the script, he gave the answers to their lines, if the role demanded it he even touched them, but he continued to refuse any relationship with his colleagues, so that on the stage and off it they could barely come anywhere near his stubborn solitude. The rudimentary perspicacity with which they were endowed prompted them to give all this the name of mourning, and at the nightly reunions in the restaurant they wondered how long it would take for Vulpius to resign himself to the inevitable and return to live upon this earth. But although they did not dare to admit it, they were not very impatient for this to happen; if as they were lamenting the young actor's absence he had suddenly come into the restaurant and sat down at the table they shared, they would probably not have endured the gloom of it without losing their good humour and they would not have been able to go on eating with the same appetite.

XXV

THUS, EVER MORE UNREACHABLE, Vulpius sank deeper by the day into his madness. Every voice around him had been hushed, and he saw nothing of the charms that life can offer, gripped as he was by the monotonous scansion of the stage rite. He was seldom seen any more outside the theatre; his colleagues suspected that he spent the whole night there, that he sometimes even slept there, as suggested by the crumpled cover of the divan which someone looking from the threshold of his dressing-room might fleetingly glimpse. The cleaning-women nearly always found the door locked, and if they knocked they were answered by the chilly voice of the young actor saying that he did not wish to be disturbed at that moment; they should come back later, or better still not come back at all, he himself would see to it that things were tidied up.

Often he left in the corridor some wrapping-paper containing the remains of a hasty meal: cheese rinds, peach and cherry stones, at the most the leftovers of one of those instant light dishes sold by the delicatessen, and the sturdy women workers would pick it up with a shake of the head, muttering that a lot more was needed for sustenance and that the gentleman was making a serious mistake feeding himself with snacks like this instead of eating properly. An opinion shared by the actors, who, however, refrained from any further attempts at persuading Vulpius to change his regime. They would only have wasted their breath on someone who listened to nobody, and it was now extremely hard even to gain admission to his presence. Anyway, it was his loss, going a bit hungry certainly wouldn't do him any harm, and even if those nibbles were not very substantial the airs that he gave himself would have been enough to puff him up amply. Some live on roast meat and some live on pride; Vulpius had obviously chosen to belong to the second category, and if he was happy like that they had no complaint to make about it.

It should be made clear that this heartlessness was the result of repeated disenchantments, of numerous fruitless efforts and expressions of concern rewarded only by a curt response. Besides, it is not at all surprising that the actors and the staff preferred to have as little as possible to do with this strange character when even I, albeit conscious of my obligations as the narrative voice, sometimes feel the need to step some distance away from him and linger over the figures who surround him, who are all the more reassuring in their normality. Yet, as I have already said, adopting the perspective of these figures is not the way to make great progress upon the necessary path the story has to follow, and in the end we only find ourselves in front of the dressing-room door, locked to keep out curious eyes by a Vulpius who is increasingly solitary and jealous of his solitude.

But to us it is granted to pass beyond that door; there is no precaution to be sustained against our omniscient gaze, and however much he believes himself to be unobserved we can see him very well as he sits in front of the mirror, staring at his own reflection, and he is so absorbed that he hears none of the sounds likely to be coming from the corridor. Knowing whether it is morning, afternoon or evening does not matter: at any hour we would discover him fully made up; a layer of greasepaint covers his face at all times and thick lines drawn with a black pencil emphasise the outlines of his eyes. It is a mask which is never taken off, not even before going to bed, and when he makes his entrance on stage he only needs a little retouching to be ready to play his part. Only in the event of his rare outings does he decide to remove his make-up with a napkin, but the sight of his own face naked strikes him as singularly unpleasant. He now has the feeling that he cannot survive except in the realms of artifice, that he runs the risk of dissolving as soon as he draws aside from it, as if the mask itself were the face, the only real one, and the lineaments which it hides only a paltry and insignificant support.

There must be someone in the theatre, if we see Vulpius not on the stage but shut away in his dressing-room; for he takes refuge there only to protect himself from those invasions. He can barely tolerate them, and if there is still something in this bizarre existence of his which is comparable to happiness, it is what he feels when he hears the others leave and he can look forward to hours of total peace in the empty theatre. However much actors and members of the audience believe they have a right to disturb his tranquillity with importunate visits and even the cleaning-women thoughtlessly violate the silence of that sanctuary by padding up and down the corridor with buckets and floorcloths, their presence seems to him transitory and bereft of reality, like a tumult of ghosts. In there he alone is real, to him alone does the theatre belong as some true, exclusive possession, because Vulpius has become for his part an exclusive possession of the theatre; the foyer and the dressing-rooms, the hall glittering with gold and the meanders understage, are bound to him no less closely than his own body, forming the organs and the limbs of the new individual who gradually, throughout solitary vigils and long days of contemplation, has taken the place of the young actor Vulpius, of that ridiculous, irresolute creature ruled by the illusion of existing on his own account. Now he knows instead that he is the focus in which converge the beams of a fiction. If the spotlights were to go out he would disappear immediately, if he left the stage he would find nothing waiting for him except perhaps what awaited Dora, who was too naive and presumptuous when she tried to deny her nature by running away from the theatre. This awareness should appal him, whereas it inspires him with comfort and even a certain mournful enthusiasm. After all it is no mean privilege to occupy the only spot of light in a pitch-dark universe, and it matters little that the light is artificial; he would certainly not exchange it for the false reality of the sun that shines outside, becoming more aggressive as the season goes on, in whose glimmer the others ignorantly bathe. They seek its warmth, are gladdened by the near-summer climate that already pervades the city, animating its streets with an eager, noisy life; but he prefers to keep apart and go on sensing that touch of ice from which the theatre has not yet freed itself, that biting reminder which penetrates his very bones, especially at night, as Vulpius faces the empty hall from the stage.

XXVI

ALTHOUGH VULPIUS REFUSED TO be drawn into it, remaining stubbornly fixed upon the neutral season of the theatre, hardly seeing any sky but that which covered the hall with the immutable rigidity of the stuccoes, outside spring advanced by leaps and bounds towards summer, the vegetation in the parks becoming increasingly opulent, exhausted by the weight of its own luxuriance, and the ladies of good society were already looking forward to the approaching holidays. For now no one was prepared to miss the few attractions the city still offered in that scrap of spring, among which the performances at the Municipal Theatre played an altogether not insignificant part. When the very last work in the programme had brightly overcome the test of opening night by earning a moderate but unblemished success, the superintendent breathed a sigh of relief and set about closing a balance-sheet that was as usual in the black, and the actor-manager congratulated himself, not without sharing his satisfaction with all those in earshot, for having once more hit on the right choice of programme, in spite of the pedants and the malicious, allowing the little ship he commanded happily to reach port through the perilous sea of public opinion.

As the time of summer closure came closer, lines were being delivered with a certain weariness, in an atmosphere of demobilisation to which only Vulpius remained insensible. Deaf to the audience's applause and yet furiously committed to the strenuous exercise of his own talent, he continued living in the theatre and for the theatre, and if on the increasingly rare occasions when his colleagues managed to exchange a few words with him they alluded to their holiday plans he seemed not even to understand what they were talking about. And yet he waited for the season to end with impatience, even with a euphoria which he had difficulty in concealing. One day he came upon his colleagues in the leading actor's dressing-room intent on considering the accuracy of some brochures in which the boarding-houses and hotels of a tourist resort promised their clients comfortable rooms and rich, varied menus. When they saw him appear they stopped and gave him a welcoming look, but he turned his eyes away and went off, saying nothing; then they resumed their discussion, glad of their narrow escape; if Vulpius wanted to keep to himself, so much the better; they asked nothing more than to be rid of this depressing colleague, at least during the holidays. Knowing him to be all alone moved them to pity and so they were willing to have him tag along, but to all appearances the person in question did not at all appreciate this willingness, so let him stay in the city and stew in his own juice or let him go and spend the summer where it pleased him best, maybe in a monastery of Trappist monks; nobody there would disturb his precious concentration in an effort to get chatting. Not that it was the ideal solution, for the presence of the monks, silent though it was, did not guarantee perfect privacy. It would be better to imagine him in the middle of the desert, perched on a pillar like a stylite, and casting contemptuous looks down on earthly wretchedness. But it could be that that kind of pillar no longer existed, and anyway there were no deserts in that part of the world – to find one he would have to get to the sea and board a steamer; thing was, with what he was paid as an actor the distinguished colleague would have trouble allowing himself the luxury of being an anchorite.

This sarcasm concealed genuine concern for the Vulpius of old and at the same time it served as an outlet for the irritation aroused in them by the arrogant Vulpius who had replaced him. It was intolerable seeing him going round looking like someone who is thinking: 'How much longer are you going to be in my way?' or barricading himself superciliously in his dressing-room. They had often been tempted to come out with it and give him a piece of their mind, but when they remembered the tragedy of Dora they restrained themselves so as not to hit out at a man already so stricken by suffering. This was their stated reason, at any rate; in reality,

what made them so meek was to a large extent
the peculiar uneasiness he inspired in them and as the
weeks went by this gradually altered into dread, as
if before an incomprehensible creature who in his
incomprehensibility was vaguely threatening.

I doubt whether Vulpius realised that he provoked
such feelings, and even had he noticed he would
probably not have bothered to dispel them; all that
mattered to him was to be left in peace, to be distracted as little as possible from his febrile
concentration; apart from this, they could think
whatever they wanted about him. In the world
where he now lived, cordiality and enmity, mutual
regard and deliberate wounding, meanness and courtesy and everything else that can intervene in a
normal co-existence between human beings lost all
significance. Drastic shunning of all affection was an
indispensable condition for being admitted into this
world, which was attained only singly, once success
had been achieved in silencing the chatter of daily
life within oneself. At least so it seemed to Vulpius,
who day after day applied these precepts with
inflexible rigour, as if he wanted to purge himself of
his own earthly substance; his colleagues were not
far off the mark with their joking references to
monks and anchorites, for in his way he really did
practise a kind of mystical exaltation in order to
turn himself into a living nonentity, into a totally
empty, passive receptacle.

In this atmosphere of mutual coldness the night
of the final performance was reached. It was the
end of June. The ladies had already left their resi-

dences in town for their holiday homes, so that in the stalls and in the boxes very few female figures with their colourful outfits interrupted the black-and-white monotony of dinner jackets and shirt-fronts. By contrast, the gallery was crowded with spectators of both sexes who, unable to seek new entertainments among the worldly pleasures of a tourist resort, viewed with dismay the closure of the theatre and the months of forced abstinence that awaited them. Their enjoyment of the last bright spot in the season, although thinly veiled with a touch of melancholy, was all the greater, and when the curtain went down there was no end to their applause nor to their noisily expressed enthusiasm, which, rather than for the play, was for the theatre itself, an institution whose importance for collective wellbeing never seemed as plain and indisputable as when they were compelled to give it up.

The actors experienced not dissimilar feelings, and one of the women, retreating into the wings between one curtain call and the next, even had to have recourse to a handkerchief to hold back the liquid outburst of emotion and limit its disastrous effects on her stage make-up. But even those who were not easily moved to tears wondered with sudden bewilderment what they would do for all that time, how would they fill their days, because in the long run distraction eventually produces deadly boredom and if one rests over time one actually becomes exhausted. As they listened to the roar of the applause they missed it in advance and regretted that dignity forbade them to seek a summer engagement in the little theatre of some spa resort. Only Vulpius seemed immune from such dejection; he made his exits and entrances on stage, bowing to the audience with his usual detachment, and the gaze he turned on the brightly chandelier-lit hall was anything but one of farewell.

XXVII

SEVERAL WEEKS HAVE PASSED since that night and no hubbub enlivens the boarding-house corridors now; plunged in perplexed stillness, the bedrooms await the return of their occupants, and in the ground-floor dining-room the shared table has been dismembered into many little tables where occasional clients sometimes sit. The days advance slowly beneath a stagnant sky that is forever dimmed by soft vapours; to escape this sultriness, whoever is able remains indoors during the hottest hours, so that the whole city appears depopulated just like the boarding-house, paralysed by a heavy torpor from which it rouses itself only towards evening, when the sun, close to setting, subdues its fierce, burning heat and a cooler air comes down from the hills. Then everybody pours out into the streets, vying with one another for the little open-air tables of the cafés and pastry shops, joining endless queues at the roadside stalls to procure a slice of watermelon or an ice-cream cone, and until late into the night the town-centre thoroughfares are filled with the good-natured atmosphere of some country festival to which the pavement musicians will furnish the necessary musical accompaniment in exchange for a few coins.

Anyone passing through the theatre square at such a time would face a dark frontage with its doors barred shut and would have trouble recognising the enticing spot where only last month at the same hour long ranks of motor cars and carriages lined up, and ladies and gentlemen fleetingly paraded their evening attire before disappearing again through the great luminous archways. All this seemed to belong to a remote era; abandonment gave the theatre an air of severity, almost surliness, and no clearer contrast could have been imagined than with the benign elegance of old or the commonplace festivities which now laid siege to it.

To such eyes it would have been unimaginable that a single soul was left in that hermetically sealed theatre. Even the cleaning-women had weeks since discontinued their now superfluous work, leaving the spiders to weave their webs in blessed peace and the dust to gather undisturbed until the autumn. Thus for a couple of months no one would set foot in the theatre, or at least this was the generally held belief of staff and common citizens; we, however, are authorised to harbour some doubts about this, since we can remember that Vulpius kept the key to the stage door like some precious possession and we can also remember that he had looked forward to the season's ending with eager impatience.

If we take a few steps backwards, as far as the day when even those actors who have lingered on longest in town left the boarding-house for their holiday destination, we can see him at the window of his bedroom, half hidden behind the curtains, his eyes on the street, where trunks and suitcases are being loaded one after the other into the luggage compartment of a taxi cab. Ever since the curtain had fallen on the last night of the run, he had had to stop his visits to the theatre almost completely so as not to attract the attention of the staff busy tidying up before the summer break, and he had spent a period of exile made all the more painful by the difficulty of avoiding the indiscreet watchfulness of his colleagues. But now at last the theatre had closed its doors and he remained alone in town; he watched the travellers get into their motorcar and lean out of the windows to give a friendly wave to the boarding-house landlady, who stood erect before the threshold looking on as her guests left; the vehicle moved off, bumpily at first, then headed smoothly towards the station.

Barely had it turned the first corner when Vulpius stepped away from the window, relieved by the thought that there was nobody now to pay heed to his movements. He had already informed the boarding-house owner that he too would soon be going on holiday, and for the past two days he had been busy getting ready. He had to take some luggage with him in order not to arouse suspicion, so he had piled shirts and articles of linen higgledy-piggledy into a suitcase. Moreover he had taken care to settle his bill, saying that he intended to be away for a very long time and preferred not to leave anything outstanding; he had not yet fixed on the date for his return, but he would send a telegram to give due warning.

The very next morning, around four, when the cheerful hurly-burly of the summer night had long since subsided and not the faintest sound came from the deserted streets, Vulpius left the boarding-house with his suitcase in his hand and the key in one of his jacket pockets and unobserved travelled the short road that separated him from the theatre. In front of the stage door he looked around to make sure he was not seen, then, with his heart beating strangely, he turned the key in the lock and slipped into the darkness of the corridor. Only when he had closed the door again, triple-locking it, did he remember to breathe. Now I am safe, he thought, now they cannot find me. He turned on the light and walked forward; in the dressing-rooms the faded wallpaper was no longer enlivened by the colours of the costumes hanging up, the tops of dressing-tables were cleared and in front of the mirrors there no longer shone the delicate opalescence of bottles and flagons; maybe it was the actors themselves, maybe the cleaning-women, who had destroyed those fragile charms, installing in their place a rigorous and bleak order. And yet, like this too, it was his abode, and with a sense of joyous headiness Vulpius savoured the knowledge that he could relish it alone for a time that seemed to him limitless.

He set the suitcase in his dressing-room and sat

down to draw breath. He had walked hurriedly, almost running, and the excitement too had taken his breath away, yet he could not manage to stay still for long; he had to make sure the theatre was really inviolable, so he set himself the task of inspecting the doors that led outside. Every last one of them was closed, thank heavens, with an abundance of bolts and bars. It worried him a little that there were others who also owned keys, but his mind was set at rest almost at once: both the superintendent and the actor-manager were out of town, and who but them would have ventured to enter unless for some serious reason?

Hot and exhausted, he went back to his dressing-room. Water still flowed from the tap of his wash-basin, first in drips, then in a gushing rusty stream, and Vulpius bathed his wrists and temples. He would soon get used to this stifling atmosphere – he would have to get used to it, for there was no way he could even consider opening cracks to let in a little air. No, he had to endure this, and would have endured it very well had he been less tired. He had spent the night without sleeping a wink, unable even to stay in bed, his state of mind expectant and nervily anxious like that of someone about to keep a long-desired appointment.

Now however, once he had made himself as comfortable as possible on the uncomfortable divan, he felt his disquiet dissolve gradually and a deep calm swept through him, a tranquillity of mind and body that he had never felt before, or perhaps only in some forgotten dream of childhood. So he fell asleep easily, and if Dora had been able to see him she would not have found that slumber very different from usual: she would have perceived the same stiffness, the same rigidity of a statue, that once had so dismayed her. And yet there was something unusual that she would have seen, had she come closer: she would have noticed that Vulpius was smiling as he slept.

❖ XXVIII ❖

HE WOKE WITHOUT KNOWING how long he had slept:
the sounds of city life could not reach him
through the thick walls of the theatre, the light did
not penetrate, and on the great white clockface in
the corridor the hands days since had ceased to
mark the hours, breaking even the last link between
the time that passed on the outside and the static
time that ruled inside the deserted building.

In any case, Vulpius felt completely alert; he no
longer felt any fatigue and even the air seemed less
stifling. He rose and stretched his somewhat aching
limbs; although he was hungry he was certain he
could hold out for a long time without food, but
decided nonetheless to allow himself at least a glass
of water; he went over to the washbasin, turned on
the tap and let the water run, testing it with a finger
in the hope that it would get colder. Then he filled
the glass, downed it in big draughts, and when he
had finished drinking bent to wash his face. When
he straightened up again he saw himself in the

mirror, catching his face by surprise before it could adopt any particular expression, and in front of those still numbed features, defenceless from their lack of memory, he was struck with an obscure self-pity.

Suddenly, sharp and solid, the image of Dora came into his mind, but not as she had appeared to him in the coffin, stiffened, removed from joy and pain: he saw her walking fearfully through the streets of the nocturnal city, leaning on his arm, shivering slightly on the bare stage, her eyes seeking him out in the darkness of the stalls. That anxiety, that fragility, had always struck him as incomprehensible; yet now he found their traces within himself, faint traces which would never have induced him to retreat from his purpose and abandon the theatre, and yet enabling him, it seemed, to understand how for weaker natures it would be a comfort, even a blessing of some sort, to listen to the tinkling notes of a music box or to circle round to waltz time until the blood rose to your head and the simple, dull intoxication of being alive smothered all thought.

It was only a moment, a passing ripple on the hard surface of his resolve. He took the greasepaint out of the cabinet and with quick movements smeared it over his face, as if he was in a hurry to cover up its nakedness. Now, in the big mirror framed with shining lightbulbs, that face was altogether different, it was a strange and inanimate object, and Vulpius could look at it with detachment as expert touches transformed it little by little into a mask.

When he had finished he went down under the stage, and among the trunks neatly ranged along the wall of the wardrobe room he sought the one containing the costumes for *Don Juan*. He opened it and began turning back the edges of the covers that protected the clothes until he found Sganarelle's livery. With this he completed his metamorphosis, stripping off his everyday garb and putting on the long white stockings, the knee breeches, the braided jacket; then he slipped on the patent-leather shoes and tied the high linen ruff round his neck. Looking at him now we might have the feeling that we were being taken back to the beginnings of our story, to the moment when Vulpius was getting ready to go on stage for the opening performance, yet in that pinched face, in that wooden figure, there is no longer anything that recalls Sganarelle's vivacity, his winks and his naive cunning. We must not let ourselves be deceived by the costume; the role which Vulpius is about to play is of a radically different kind, one to which the waxy patina spread over his face by powder and greasepaint is well suited: still the role of a servant, we might say, but a servant who does not expect his wages from any noble of Seville or punished rake. If need be, I could bring to mind that on that far-off night a performance other than the one anticipated by the programme was enacted, a comedy of looks, a drama with no epilogue silently wrought between the box and the stage, and venture the fairly plausible surmise that Vulpius had the intention of bringing one of its protagonists to life again.

All this has an air of verisimilitude, if I may be allowed to use a term whose aptness in relation to Vulpius I doubted at the start, and which it is now perhaps legitimate to reclaim with a new meaning. There is verisimilitude in the possibility that this character will continue, determinedly, right to the end of the road along which we have seen him proceed, and that this path is not a straight line where everything vanishes without trace, to be superseded by other things, but a circle where every-thing, sooner or later, is destined to return. Neither the laws of narrative nor those of madness are fond of dispersal, preferring to mix and remix a limited number of elements until the circle closes. Now, it is certainly no mystery that this story is approaching its conclusion; you can tell just from seeing how many pages are left. Which means that it really is time, it is right that things should come round again: Sganarelle's costume, but perhaps also the unknown woman's watch and the black satin mask which Vulpius, our indispensable accomplice in the act of reminiscence, could have slipped into his suitcase before making his way to the theatre and then set down somewhere, in a drawer or more likely in full view, to direct the steps he was to take under the guidance of these unpropitious talismans. Objects and thoughts, images perceived and remembered, return like the themes in musical dramas, mingling, composing a whole, revealing correspondences, and we attend their systematic re-emergence through the gestures enacted by Vulpius in the empty theatre.

Reality has always been in short supply in here,

and now it seems that there is none at all; even Vulpius, proceeding stiffly and slowly towards the stage in his seventeenth-century outfit, resembles anything but a real creature, and we are almost astounded to find a quickened breath, the beating of a heart, under the jacket that clasps his chest like a cuirass. But this is of minor importance, or at least he thinks so: a tiny flaw in the otherwise perfect domain of the masquerade, the only one which matters, the only one where all the scattered fragments of his destiny can at last be joined. And Vulpius sets the stage with care, turning on the spotlights, angling the beams so that they do not wholly dissolve the darkness in which it is plunged but create within it, at the very centre, only a glimmering island, a clearly defined strip that runs from the front of the stage all the way to the backdrop. Then he steps away, goes back down understage and from here reaches the warehouse where furnishings, properties and rolled-up scenery are piled together; he rummages for a long time through these obsolete worlds in search of his own, chooses its essential components and conveys them onto the stage, one after another: two trestles and a long rough wooden table. He arranges the trestles so that they are parallel to the front of the stage, sets the table across them, then steps back a few paces to check that this position is the one he wants. Yes, he is satisfied, but he is a little out of breath, and his heartbeat has got louder and more irregular again, as it did when the door of the theatre gaped open in front of him a few hours ago, or it could have been many hours

ago. A small flaw, an imperfection without significance: he only has to stop for a minute or two and
take deep breaths and his agitation will calm down,
for the agitation is not his but only that of his heart,
his blood, his body, that unruly mechanism which
opposes his purposes with its own, yet which he
does not doubt he will succeed in dominating.

He lets his gaze run from one end of the hall to
the other, dwelling on the caryatids and cupids, on
the crimson draperies and the dimmed lustre of the
stuccoes, seeking the support of these mute allies.
And it really does seem to him that he draws
strength from everything surrounding him, that he
is given ultimate approval by an authority before
which nothing remains except surrender and obedience. Let his blood and breath surrender, then, let
them obey, and the sudden troublesome memory
of everything that exists outside these walls, of the
countless lures, so flimsy yet so enticing, of which
the life of men is made; but what charm does the
world have to offer that can outdo the burning
splendour of the stage lights? The world that would
await him outside is a murky one, an approximate
world that lacks the courage of falsehood, the
courage of truth. When he arrived and locked the
door behind him, Vulpius already knew that he
would never again agree to perform a role in it,
indeed he knew this much earlier, and now fear, the
resurgence of dull and rudimentary impulses attempt
in vain to shake his intransigence. Here is the stage
and this is the role that is his, the only possible one,
the only comprehensible one. Wrenching a smile

from him, there comes into his mind the image of the leading actor on New Year's Eve, tipsy with champagne, as he stood up on those very same boards defending his actor's pride against the profane; and even this unexpected association does not displease him (as it does not displease me), for into the best tragedies the threads of farce are inextricably woven and he himself has chosen to wear the garb of a buffoon to go up on that stage.

Now he is calm, completely calm. He feels as if he has faced and defeated a multitude of ghosts, those who, in the fifth act, the night before the battle, come one by one to the protagonist's tent as if it were visiting time. 'Despair and live,' they told him, or else 'Hope and live,' but he did not listen to their voices, and Dora too, the most dangerous apparition, with her heartrending accompaniment of waltzes and tinkling music, ostrich plumes and dented shooting stars, has been overthrown by a different Dora, a statue among statues, around which there rise clouds of incense and solemn Latin phrases.

This image gets increasingly close, becomes increasingly present, as Vulpius goes back down into the bowels of the theatre and re-emerges carrying a black cloth in his arms. His is an abstract, stylised performance, it does not indulge in the facile decorative tendencies to which the actor-manager so often resorts in his props; for this reason he has not even bothered to see whether in the jumble of objects filling the warehouse, among that chaos before the Creation, there might perchance be some candlesticks or a papier-mâché tabernacle to put before the audience during scenes of weddings, coronations, fatal encounters in church between devout young girls and their future seducers. Doubtless had he searched he would have found something of the kind, but he has no need of it; he prefers to make do with the black cloth, which he spreads out across the table, careful in his draping of its edges, so that the richness of the fabric is arrayed, especially on the side visible from the stalls. When he deems it arranged in the best possible way he climbs up onto the catafalque, stretches out on it, folds his hands on his chest, where his heart responds to the pressure with a timid, resigned beating. Thus he remains, supine and motionless, thus he means to remain, until that rebel body turns to stone and the statues welcome it into their triumphant community. Now his lips are slightly parted in a frozen ecstasy, his tightly closed eyelids become increasingly heavy, but Vulpius does not need to open his eyes to know that the woman watcher is staring at him from the proscenium box.

Also published by Serpent's Tail

Artemisia by Anna Banti
Translated by Shirley Caracciolo

NOW A MAJOR FILM

'It is astonishing that this novel, published in Italy in 1947, has never before been translated into English, but at least the job has been superbly done. The book is beautifully produced, the translator has found the ideal voice and idiom to convey the fluency of a remarkable novel whose subject is Artemisia Gentileschi, the 17th century artist, who has become such an international feminist symbol . . . The book is a historical novel polygamously married with the essay, the biography, the autobiography and art criticism. Narrative momentum is less its *forte* than the description of random, closely observed, idiosyncratic episodes, and the brilliantly-crafted rehabilitation and re-creation of a remarkable figure. These qualities make it a bitter, passionate, intelligent and moving work which one reads with growing excitment.' *The Scotsman*

'Banti illuminates episodes from this life with an extra-ordinary telescopic clarity, as if the past really could be looked at, watched in movement, but as something very far away and out of reach. The intensity of her writing is almost unbearable at times, for underlying Artemisia's actions there is always a dynamic of painful choice, of each step taken necessitating loss as she casts off the comfort of being a loved wife, a tender mother, for the sake of artistic fulfilment.

Banti creates her quite unsentimentally as a difficult, ambitious woman of great courage, always aiming to be true to the deepest part of herself. Artemisia is a tour de force, but certain passages are of exquisite resonance: a hallucinatory sea voyage, Orazio's death, and the book's staggering final pages as Artemisia travels towards her own.' *TES*

Voices by Dacia Maraini
Translated by Dick Kitto & Elspeth Spottiswood

Michela Canova, a radio journalist, returns home to find that Angela Bari, her neighbour, has been murdered. Coincidentally, she is asked to prepare a series on crimes against women. Researching the programmes, Michela Canova is forced to confront the every day horror and violence of big city life.

Did Angela Bari, seemingly so sweet and fragile, drive her many admirers to the very limit of sexual frenzy until one of them exploded in an orgy of hatred and loathing? And why does she, Michela Canova, see the same pattern of incitement and repulsion repeat itself in her own relationships?

Once again, Dacia Maraini asks fundamental questions about the human condition. How much can individuals escape patterns of domination, of male domination, that are in place the world over? Her sophisticated answers show why Maraini is one of Europe's outstanding voices.

'Maraini's great skill is that she does not allow the exploration of ideas to take over at the expense of the story, nor the story to obscure the ideas.' *The Independent on Sunday*

'An artist of considerable power.' *The Scotsman*

'Italy's most audacious writer.' *The Sunday Times*

The Way Back by Enrico Palandri
Translated by Stuart Hood

'In Bologna I got out of the train with my suitcase, convinced I had to change trains, I went to the bar and when I heard the departure announced ran back to the platform in time only to see the last coach with its fine sign *Rome* whiz past under my nose and to watch the bits of paper pirouetting on the rails in the draught. The next fast train is in an hour. I sat in the waiting-room; in front of me I have the memorial tablet for the massacre of the second of August nineteen eighty, I read the names of the dead, then an article I found in the train and meantime look at the people in the rooom. I think of someone who on that second of August had missed a connection, maybe someone like me . . .'

The Way Back is a novel of exile and return. It is the story of Davide, an Italian psychiatrist, and his Scottish wife, Julia, a singer. Travelling back to Rome from London, Davide sees before him memories of his generation: his childhood and family, political dissent and terrorism, elected exile and yearning for his native land. The peculiar prerogative of the émigré is seen to be an absolute clarity of mind where self and country are concerned.

Beautifully written and hauntingly moving, *The Way Back* is among the most impressive Italian novels of the past few years.

'The political and the private domain intertwine, producing despair in the political arena but hope in the personal domain. The overlay of present on past is skilfully handled, as are Palandri's thoughtful insights, his storytelling talents, his deftly constructed characters and sensitive play with the emotions. It is an impressive work by an interesting young writer.' *The Scotsman*